24 François Truffaut

François Truffaut

Don Allen

The Viking Press
New York

The Cinema One series is published by
The Viking Press in association with
the British Film Institute

Published in 1974 in a hardbound and paperbound
edition by
The Viking Press, Inc.,
625 Madison Avenue, New York, N.Y. 10022

SBN 670–32707–7 (hardbound)
SBN 670–01975–5 (paperbound)

Library of Congress catalog card number: 73–14080

Printed and bound in Great Britain

Contents

Cover: *La Nuit Américaine* (Jean-Pierre Léaud and François Truffaut)

Introduction

This book is intended as an affectionate yet critical study of the films of François Truffaut. The success of the book as a whole depends largely on the extent to which I have succeeded in tempering the warmth of my admiration with the coolness of my critical judgments.

I make no apology for the essentially subjective nature of the value judgments contained in this work; they seem to me inevitable in a study of this kind. I have tried to argue my opinions and to illustrate them from the films, but film criticism, despite current emphasis on what seems to me the myth of an objective, structured approach, is ultimately the result of subjective likes and dislikes which have coalesced into 'personal taste'. The best the critic can do is to state his bias and his approach and leave the rest to the reader.

I have assumed that most readers will have seen most of Truffaut's films but not all of them. Therefore I have worked some kind of plot résumé into each chapter. The chronological approach (with the exception of the four films in the Antoine Doinel cycle) and the allocation of one chapter per film may be useful for the reader who wishes to study one film in isolation. The danger of this method is to focus attention on the individual film rather than on the *oeuvre* as a whole, with consequent loss of continuity and thematic unity. I have tried to offset this by emphasizing recurring themes in the films and by drawing attention to the echoes and resonances – of a personal, literary and cinematic nature – which permeate Truffaut's whole work. Thus although the Antoine Doinel films are considered together, because of the obvious autobiographical links (which I have discussed in Chapter Four by means of a limited examination of what

Truffaut on the set of *Fahrenheit 451*, with Cyril Cusack and Bee Duffell little evidence there is available on Truffaut's private life) this grouping should not blind us to the strong autobiographical thread running through the whole body of Truffaut's films. In an interview in *Le Monde* (25 November 1971), Truffaut even considers that he is more intimate and sincere in the films outside the Antoine Doinel cycle: 'I have a great tendency to talk of myself, and a very great revulsion against doing so directly.'

So Truffaut's films are always about himself; to a greater or lesser extent, less obviously in some films than in others, but nevertheless always. They are also always about love, again with a similar caveat. These elements are of course not mutually exclusive, but are combined in different ways from film to film. The typical Truffaut hero contains many of Truffaut's own personal characteristics *and* is involved in some sort of 'love' relationship. These two recurring preoccupations are announced in Truffaut's first film, *Les Mistons*, and have been taken up repeatedly throughout his work.

The two major themes may be variously subdivided. For example, the importance of friendship, especially male friendship; the role of women – dream goddesses, mother figures or whores; the intoxication with cinema and especially with the American B-film, to which many innuendoes and jokes refer; the fascination with language, as an instrument of or aid to communication.

The view of life which seems to me to emerge from the films (almost, one feels, without Truffaut being aware of it) is one of profound pessimism. Take, for instance, the ambiguity of his stance in connection with *L'Enfant Sauvage*. His apparent approval of the partially successful attempt to civilize the wild child, and his total endorsement in interviews of the desirability of the experiment, are out of harmony with the reaction of many spectators, who would question both the aims and methods of an experiment based on the assumption that a being forcibly indoctrinated by nineteenth-century pedagogy was likely to be happier than a 'savage' in his natural state. Truffaut seems not to have considered this alternative view.

In other films Truffaut is aware of the atmosphere of despair and makes conscious efforts to avert it by deliberately lightening the tone. The interpolation of very funny comic banter from the two ludicrous heavies in *Tirez sur le Pianiste* into a melodramatic love story involving two deaths – one caused by them – is the most disturbing example of this mixing of tones. Here the film works, probably because of the bitter-sweet juxtaposition; though this does not prevent the overriding melancholy from seeping through.

Pessimism about the human condition is a factor in most of Truffaut's films. 'L'amour fou', absolute and unconditional, is not of this earth (Fabienne Tabard and also the 'man in the mac' in *Baisers Volés*, and Louis' feelings for Marion in *La Sirène du Mississippi*). The compromises which are possible may be encompassed within the frustrating limitations of marriage (notably in *La Peau Douce, Fahrenheit 451* and *Domicile Conjugal*), or in the couple relationship outside marriage (*La Peau Douce, Antoine et Colette, Baisers Volés,* etc.), or in the magnificent failure of the threesome in *Jules et Jim* and *Les Deux Anglaises et le Continent*. In more than half of the films, death comes to at least one of the lovers; in most of them, one character is left alone at the end. The celebrated 'open endings' are perhaps less open than they seem – Truffaut is reluctant to emphasize the potentially tragic isolation of the individual survivors, or the potential boredom of the couples. The conclusion, in Truffaut's own words, is that, 'The couple solution does not work and there are no other solutions.' Perhaps he should now go on to investigate the possibilities of the extended family in the literary commune at the end of *Fahrenheit 451*.

This book attempts to show Truffaut's obsessive preoccupation with these recurring themes; it will be justified if it thus reveals Truffaut to be a film author as worthy of study as any of the directors discovered by him and his *Cahiers du Cinéma* colleagues in the Fifties. At the moment Truffaut is a relatively unfashionable source of study. His limitations are so apparent; his interest in developing new cinematic techniques is virtually non-existent; he is content mainly to use existing procedures for his own purposes. With rare exceptions his films are 'well made' and tell a story. His emphasis tends to be on narrative and character study, which explains why this book is also concerned with these aspects. Many of Truffaut's adaptations from existing sources have a pronounced 'literary' flavour, far removed from the chimerical 'visual purity' demanded by some critics. There is a marked absence of actuality in his films (Truffaut never votes and only fairly recently discovered the joys of reading *Le Monde*). There is almost no evidence of any serious political awareness in his films, and only limited, and purely marginal, social comment. Many contemporary critics dismiss him as a bourgeois anachronism who has been left behind by the currents of his time.

There is an element of truth in these criticisms; sufficient, it seems to me, to make it clear that Truffaut is not a major artist with an all-embracing, cosmic vision of the human condition, nor one who will exercise a revolutionary influence upon our times or even upon the cinema. Yet Truffaut is important almost *because* of his limitations and the small scale on which he works. Monsieur Tabard in *Baisers Volés*, a neurotic, repressed fascist with a persecution complex, defends Hitler against Madame Tabard's jibe that he was a house-painter with the injured assertion that he was a 'petit peintre pays-agiste'. The same defence, in serious vein, might be made of Truffaut. His 'landscape' is reduced to the human level; his portraits are concerned with the minute fluctuations of emotion, the ebb and flow of confidence, timidity, affection, desire. He will allow no criticism of the subject-matter of his films and fiercely asserts his right to film only what interests him passionately, subjects in which he has immersed himself for months or even years before shooting begins. Hence the immensely personal, bitter-sweet, nostalgic tone of much of his work. Truffaut's canvas may be that of a miniaturist, but within his chosen range he is a master.

1: Grave-digger to Film-maker

This above all to thine own self be true.
And it must follow as the night the day,
Thou canst not then be false to any man.
Hamlet

Some misconceptions about the work of Truffaut the film-maker arise directly from the career of Truffaut the critic. And Truffaut's formative years as a critic are a necessary point of departure in any assessment of his films. In 1952, thanks especially to the help of his mentor and surrogate father André Bazin, Truffaut was appointed film critic for the French cultural magazine *Arts*, and also began to write regularly for *Cahiers du Cinéma*. Thus began the flow of articles, reviews and interviews which deluged the French intellectual public in the late Fifties and early Sixties, diminishing, as Truffaut's own film output increased, to the occasional article in *Cahiers* by the late Sixties.

In the mid-Fifties, together with his *Cahiers* colleagues Doniol-Valcroze, Rohmer, Rivette, Godard and Chabrol, Truffaut saw much to destroy. Passionately, flamboyantly, he set about destroying it. He became known as 'the grave-digger of the French cinema', hated by those he attacked, revered and esteemed by those who shared his views. In 1958 Doniol-Valcroze said of him: 'In a few years François Truffaut has become the most famous of the young film critics. What many muttered under their breaths he dared to say out loud ... He has firmly kicked the conformist backside of the French cinema.'

The main target for Truffaut's toe was the hidebound French cinema of the Forties and early Fifties. An unequivocal one-line notice, 'In not seeing *Chéri-Bibi* you will doubtless spend an excellent evening,' a provocative 'There is nothing more to say of *Futures Vedettes* except that the French cinema will produce many more films of this "non-quality" until the public learns to choose and

11

Father figures: André Bazin (with Alexandre Astruc), Jean Renoir and Alfred
Hitchcock

eventually to smash the seats,' sufficed to dismiss the dross. The gold was to be found among the seventeen directors Truffaut had placed in the 'ambitious' section of his classification of ninety-nine French directors, which he drew up in 1955. The other three sections consisted of the 'semi-ambitious', the 'honourably commercial' and the 'deliberately commercial'. This rigid schematization did not, however, ensure automatic praise even for the seventeen directors in Truffaut's personal pantheon.

Truffaut's invective frequently involved quite vicious personal attacks. In a review of *Chiens perdus sans collier* (1955), he wrote: 'The whole is written to order for the Gaumont-Palace by two disillusioned and cynical scriptwriters – Jean Aurenche and Pierre Bost, who have written "touching" dialogue – and is set to images by a man insufficiently intelligent to be cynical, too crafty to be sincere, too pretentious and solemn to be simple, Jean Delannoy.' Claude Autant-Lara was similarly pilloried, not merely for his 'truculence, vulgarity, exaggeration' and his resemblance to a butcher who persists in doing fine embroidery, but also, and particularly, because he is only a diligent *metteur en scène* of scripts written by others; he is not a film author but an 'illustrator of texts'. 'Autant pour Lara', one of Truffaut's more forgettable puns, was the punchline to this particular polemic.

The word 'revolutionary' might be applied to Truffaut in two senses only. First because he was committed to the violent destruction by spectacular critical attacks of what he judged bad; secondly, and more literally, because 'revolution' for him has implied turning the wheel back to his cinematic golden age, the Thirties. The cinema which Truffaut advocates is firmly based on the best characteristics of this period, and in particular on the total authorship and consequent directorial freedom of such lyrical film creators as Jean Renoir and Jean Vigo. Truffaut alternates vigorous attacks on partial creators and production line commercialists with equally militant defence of independent film-makers. It was largely as a result of the perceptive exegeses and initial pioneering publicity of Truffaut and his *Cahiers* colleagues that American directors such as Hawks, Walsh and Fuller, who had formerly been identified in the public mind, if at all, as part of the Hollywood machine, were raised to *auteur* status. In addition, an enthusiasm was generated for the American B-picture, which was to exercise a strong influence on

13

The American connection: gangster film pastiche in *Tirez sur le Pianiste*

Truffaut and Godard in particular and to provide them with the framework and background for several of their films. In Truffaut's case, *Tirez sur le Pianiste*, *La Mariée était en noir* and *La Sirène du Mississippi* are inconceivable without his exposure to the American cinema in the late Forties and the Fifties. Together with *Fahrenheit 451*, these films constitute what might be called the 'American' strand in Truffaut's work. They reflect predominantly the influence of Hollywood and in particular of Hitchcock, though the Hitchcockian influence is discernible in other films. The rest of Truffaut's work, particularly the Antoine Doinel films, might be regarded as part of the French lyrical tradition; and the specific influence here is Renoir.

Hitchcock is the subject of Truffaut's full-length interview book,* published in 1967 after some fifty hours of interviews

* *Hitchcock*, Simon and Schuster, New York, 1967; Secker and Warburg, London, 1968.

recorded in 1962, when Truffaut was already celebrated as a director. The book is scarcely the definitive study of Hitchcock; Truffaut has revealed greater critical insight elsewhere, notably into Hitchcock's macabre humour as revealed for example in *Rear Window*. The essential Hitchcock is never probed, remaining elusive behind the showman, raconteur, auto-publicist façade. Indeed, the main interest of the work lies in what it reveals of Truffaut's own preoccupations as a film-maker. Hitchcock, for Truffaut, emerges as the technical oracle to be consulted, the box of tricks to be ransacked. It is verification of detail, establishment of how shots and effects were achieved, which fascinates Truffaut. He has already assimilated many of the views Hitchcock expresses here, for example the fear of generating boredom, the need to entertain and therefore consciously to manipulate audience reaction. When the occasional disagreement does emerge, Truffaut is too reticent and Hitchcock too experienced at interviews for the point to be forced home. Hitchcock's outright commercialism is never challenged, nor his dismissal of the actor's role ('The chief requisite for an actor is the ability to do nothing well'). It is characteristic of a book which is more admiration than criticism that when on the penultimate page Hitchcock admits to a major weakness in his work, the 'thin characterizations within the suspense stories', Truffaut never follows it up, indeed does not even think it worthy of comment.

The evolution of the New Wave phenomenon coincided of course with the development of the *auteur* theory, and Truffaut's role in the promotion of both was decisive. The cumulative flow of his years of criticism led naturally to his 1958 manifesto, which became almost a working document for the New Wave. Studios were too expensive, so the film of tomorrow was to be shot entirely on location, in the streets, on the beaches, with natural décor and lighting; dialogue would not be the stilted and stylized product of a professional scriptwriter, but the conversation the film-maker might have had with his wife the night before, or even conversation improvised by the actors; films would be made quickly and cheaply; the film-creating process was to be demythologized so that anyone could pick up a camera and shoot a film as he might pick up a pen and write a novel. In this way a climate of opinion was established in which the New Wave could flourish. Truffaut's contribution is reflected in

Chabrol's testimony: 'Look what Truffaut has done. Things got stirred up. We all owe him a little for being able to start off as we did.'

Truffaut has remained remarkably consistent, even static, in his cinematic judgments over the past twenty years. He still defends the kind of cinema he was defending in 1955, though he has known the critic's occasional blush of shame. 'Often people quote at me some of the things I wrote and that embarrasses me greatly,' he said in connection with his oversimplification of the technical problems of film-making, which led to the excess of freewheeling camerawork, shots of beaches and sunlight, and slack editing soon to become the trademarks and the clichés of the New Wave. One inconsistency does emerge in Truffaut's attitude to the Cannes film festival. In his early days as a critic Truffaut scathingly dismissed the mediocrity of Cannes; banner headlines ('Cannes – a failure dominated by compromise, scheming and blunders') heralded a fierce denunciation of the festival which brought protests even from Henri Langlois of the French Cinémathèque and resulted in Truffaut being overlooked by the organizers of the 1957 festival; which did not stop him attending, signing his articles 'François Truffaut, the only critic not invited to the festival'. Two years later things had changed. Truffaut's first feature, *Les Quatre Cents Coups*, was shown at Cannes as the official French entry, and Truffaut accepted the Grand Prix for the film. In 1962 he was a member of the festival jury.

No one rises in a few years from anonymity to celebrity with innocence intact. But it would be misleading to accept the caricature of Truffaut as a young *arriviste* with an eye on the main chance, as some critics have done, simply because his vituperative style as a critic led to rapid public recognition and ultimately, helped by his marriage to Madeleine Morgenstern, daughter of one of France's richest and most powerful distributors, to his progress from critic to film-maker. One such critic, Henri Jeanson of *L'Aurore*, writing in 1969, accused Truffaut of merely mouthing such words as 'purity, honesty, frankness, innocence' and even claimed that '*tendresse*', the word most generally associated with Truffaut, is 'nothing but a publicity stunt'.

Truffaut certainly never disguised the fact that his intention, his dream, was to make films, and that his film reviews were increasingly an account of what he would have done with the material rather than

The New Wave at Cannes, 1959 (Truffaut on left of front row)

film criticism proper: 'I loved the cinema passionately enough not to remain a spectator.' As Doniol-Valcroze recalled in 1958: 'If he so often attacked, scorned, slandered what he did not like, it was because he wanted to do what he did like.'

A common reaction to Truffaut's films is a sense of anticlimax, prompted by the discrepancy between what Jean Curtelin has called his 'blustering declarations and his slender final baggage'. The most serious charges of all are made by those who either misunderstand or dismiss as irrelevant Truffaut's contribution to cinema. For such critics it is not enough for him to say that he did not want to change cinema but only to continue to make better examples of the kinds of film he enjoyed seeing in his youth. His indiscriminate attacks as a critic on the 'bourgeois' and 'petit bourgeois' film-makers – words which he never defined – were not surprisingly taken for authentic revolutionary language. People looked to him for committed, political films – and found him wanting. By this criterion, even if he is not the Jean Delannoy of the New Wave, he is clearly, again in the words of Curtelin, 'the *enfant terrible* confined within the bounds of bourgeois respectability'. The apparent revolutionary is only a rebel after all.

Fortunately, Truffaut's claim to originality is not affected by the absence in his films of revolutionary innovation on either a technical or a political level. He must be judged by other criteria.

2: Les Mistons

A film director's total work is a diary kept over a lifetime.
François Truffaut

Jean Renoir has said that throughout his career a director makes only one film. The others are merely remakes, reworkings of the themes contained in that first film. Truffaut subscribes to this idea, and has done consistently from his period as a critic up to the present time. And in his first film, *Les Mistons*, one finds the thematic and stylistic embryo of his later work. Truffaut himself, whose capacity for self-criticism verges on the masochistic, thinks that the critics who praised *Les Mistons* were very indulgent, and sympathetic to his intentions rather than his achievement.

Certainly the main interest of this first film lies in its germinal nature and in the light it throws on Truffaut's later work, rather than in its inherent qualities as cinema. The film was financed largely by Truffaut's wife, and shot on location at Nîmes in 1957 with the help of a few friends (notably Claude de Givray) and with five local boys as the *mistons*. Truffaut took the idea from a short story in *Les Virginales* by Maurice Pons. Despite this reliance on an existing source, and the co-operation of its author, Truffaut's adaptation emerges as the work of one man and carries his total directorial imprint.*

The film deals with the awakening sexuality of a gang of twelve-

---

* This, of course, is the essence of the *politique des auteurs* theory, as Peter Wollen has shown in *Signs and Meaning in the Cinema* (1969, Secker and Warburg, London): 'The director does not subordinate himself to another author; his source is only a pretext, which provides catalysts, scenes which fuse with his own preoccupations to produce a radically new work.'

year-old boys during a long summer in Nîmes, as they become increasingly fascinated by Bernadette, the sister of one of them, and her love affair with Gérard, 'un drôle de type' who teaches physical education at the local lycée. The boys seek to compensate for the fact that they are too young to love Bernadette by waging war on the couple, spying on them and harassing them. Gérard is killed in a climbing accident, and the film closes on a melancholy note.

The original running time of twenty-six minutes was subsequently cut by Truffaut to seventeen minutes. In this way he hoped to prune some superfluous dialogue and also to moderate the film's main weakness, which lies in the over-explicit, rather wooden commentary. This commentary reflects both Truffaut's literary origins as a film critic 'who would have written novels were it not for the cinema' and also his over-anxious desire for complete clarity in his films. But here pruning was an inadequate remedy. Tinkering about with the overstrained heart of the film is no help in a situation which calls for a transplant. The verbosity could only have been replaced by visual clarity. Hitchcock's precept, 'Whatever is said, instead of being shown, is lost upon the viewer', is here neglected by one of its firmest advocates. The ineptitude of the American paraphrased version of the commentary is a further hazard for English audiences.

Les Mistons is Truffaut's gaze through a nostalgic filter at his own and Everyman's adolescence. His personal tone permeates Maurice Pons' story, rather as Alain Resnais' individual ethos powerfully transcends each of his diverse novelist scriptwriters. In subject and mood the film closely anticipates the more directly autobiographical *Les Quatre Cents Coups*, and thus serves as a kind of preface to the Antoine Doinel cycle. It has all the awkwardness and grinding sincerity of an experimental first exercise, yet it reveals almost everything about its author: his timid, voyeuristic adoration of 'Woman'; his fondness for bitter-sweet nostalgia, in which surface humour alleviates sadness and tenderness tinges passion; a charm and lightness of touch which eschews analysis and probing; a cinematic culture underlying almost every shot and made explicit in a direct homage or an in-joke; an instinctive anticipation of audience reaction and desire to entertain, while remaining 'sincere'.

The prototype for the later diffident, vulnerable, woman-dominated Truffaut hero is to be found in the composite portrait of the *mistons*. Men are seen from the imagined viewpoint of the woman, as little boys playing games, driven on by half-understood passions, innocent victims shaped by the whim of woman, the unattainable siren and implacable love goddess. This gang of adolescents sees Bernadette as the exciting forbidden fruit, the enigmatic flower of their shameful dreams. It is not yet 'Vénus toute entière à sa proie attachée', but the symptoms are there. Incipient passion, frightening and unknown, is channelled into hatred; group solidarity emboldens faint hearts. The Don Juan syndrome asserts itself, as these former victims of the will of woman become the aggressors and begin to think in the terminology of the military campaign. The female, Bernadette, becomes the enemy; war is declared, and Truffaut unsubtly points the moral with close-ups of a female praying mantis devouring a male in copulation.

The news of Gérard's death – movingly conveyed by three superimposed dissolves of newspaper headlines (anticipating *La Sirène du Mississippi*) and a long-shot of people in mourning emerging from church (anticipating *La Mariée était en noir*) – imposes a solemnity on the end of the film. The fundamental dichotomy between lust and 'true love' is highlighted by shots of prostitutes, full-breasted women and pouting lips, intercut on three occasions with a slow-motion, almost frame by frame close-up of Gérard and Bernadette kissing in profile, an image of tenderness rendered more poignant by the recent news of his death. Then Truffaut, sensing that we are verging on tragedy, as usual lightens the mood – while retaining the thematic thread – with a shot of a voluptuous Brigitte Bardot on a poster for Vadim's *Et Dieu créa la Femme*, and in front of it a *miston* shaking his fist because the film is forbidden to those under sixteen. Other comic interludes, such as the jerkily edited, slow-motion business with the gardener and the hosepipe (a homage to Lumière) and the gag with the man who when asked for a light says aggressively that he never gives one, are simply comic relief inserts, related to nothing except Truffaut's repertoire of cinematic memories and his often expressed show business desire 'never to have two elephant acts running'. The epitome of this particular Truffaut trick is the celebrated flash shot of the gangster's mother dropping dead in *Tirez sur le Pianiste*.

The whole film can be seen as an extended homage to Jean Vigo. Not merely in its specific references to *Zéro de Conduite* in the dialogue and the camerawork (one shot of the *mistons* silhouetted against the town wall recalls Vigo's shot of the pupils in revolt on the school roof), but in its treatment of love, its gentle humour and its lyrical tone. More generally, the proliferation of cinematic allusions and cross-references with which all Truffaut's films are studded is one of the hallmarks of the New Wave. Sometimes the effect is to reinforce the theme; for example, during the obligatory cinema sequence here, when on the screen the woman in Jacques Rivette's *Le Coup du Berger* (Truffaut often plugs his friends' films) is on the point of succumbing to Jean-Claude Brialy and Truffaut cuts to Gérard and Bernadette embracing in the audience. Elsewhere the allusion takes the form of a gratuitous in-joke, for example when the *mistons* steal a poster of Jean Delannoy's *Chiens perdus sans Collier*: Truffaut, despite having previously slated the film, is still unable to let sleeping dogs lie. Other quirkily irrelevant sequences, like the bitter-sweet anecdote of Bernadette's uncle and the boil which blighted his love prospects, are included because Truffaut cannot resist them. They are on a par with the love by correspondence story in *Jules et Jim* – isolated, whimsical comments on the foibles of circumstance. Scenes such as the violent cuffing of one of the *mistons* by Gérard anticipate the striking of children in *Les Quatre Cents Coups* and *L'Enfant Sauvage* and are clearly a personal reminiscence for Truffaut, for whom adolescence was 'a bad moment to get through'.

During the winter following the shooting of *Les Mistons*, Truffaut was involved in a project which was eventually completed by Godard. The genesis of *Une Histoire d'Eau*, as this short film came to be called, could scarcely have been more casual. Always, he says, fascinated by floods, Truffaut took the opportunity of floods on the outskirts of Paris to ask Pierre Braunberger, the producer, for some spare film stock so that he could film a *fait divers* with two actors, Jean-Claude Brialy and Caroline Dim. When he got to the floods he was a little reluctant to make the film at all in view of the seriousness of the situation for the flood victims. But he shot some footage, and then did nothing more with it. Godard later took over the film, edited it, and supplied a laconic commentary. This droll, if not moral, tale is in fact co-signed by Godard and Truffaut, but Truffaut's collaboration ended with the shooting.

Influences: (*above*) Hitchcock (*La Mariée était en noir*); (*below*) Renoir (*Jules et Jim*)

23

The film chronicles the experiences of a couple cut off by the floods from the road to Paris. They talk and eventually make it (he: 'together'; she: 'to Paris'; in both senses in fact), and that is the kind of pun with which the film abounds. With its deadpan, offbeat humour, tortuous puns, intellectual asides, atmosphere of sexual amorality and mood of anarchy, the film anticipates *A Bout de Souffle*. Certainly Truffaut's sweeping camerawork, particularly the aerial shots, contributes to the fairytale atmosphere (to be recaptured in *Jules et Jim*), and, in an aside to the audience, Godard acknowledges the debt: 'Normally I don't give a damn about the image; it is the text which is important. But this time I am wrong, because here everything is beautiful.' All the same, *Une Histoire d'Eau* has Godard stamped all over it, and it cannot really be considered a Truffaut film.

3: The continuing story of Antoine Doinel

Truffaut's own statement that 'one is always autobiographical but one is so to a greater or lesser extent' can be applied more readily to himself than to most other directors. With Truffaut the autobiographical element in his work is of major importance. He is always present in his films, even though his personal appearances so far number only two – in *L'Enfant Sauvage* and, as a film director, in *La Nuit Américaine*. Sometimes he expresses and thus reveals himself through one of the minor characters; more often he does so through the hero. This is particularly the case in the Antoine Doinel cycle, with Jean-Pierre Léaud.

When interviewed, Truffaut is very reticent about the details of his private life; but from the facts that can be gleaned the parallels between his own life and that of his fictional creation overwhelmingly support the view that, at least on an autobiographical level, Antoine Doinel *is* initially François Truffaut. Like Antoine, Truffaut was an only child, had a wet-nurse and was brought up by his grandmother until the age of eight, when his parents took over, though they were too occupied with their own problems to bother much with their child. Truffaut's father's fascination with camping is echoed, in *Les Quatre Cents Coups*, the first of the Doinel films, by Monsieur Doinel's obsession with car rallies. Again, Truffaut was expelled from a succession of schools, from which he had frequently played truant and gone on clandestine trips to the cinema with his friend Robert Lachenay; Antoine does likewise with his friend René Bigey. Antoine and Truffaut both discover Balzac at an early age and are fired with an enthusiasm which continues into their adult lives.

Les Quatre Cents Coups: clandestine cinema-going (Jean-Pierre Léaud, Patrick Auffay)

Truffaut, like Antoine, committed petty crimes, ran away from school and home, lived for a time with his friend's family, was turned over to the authorities by his father, and was sent to the Reform School for Juvenile Delinquents at Villejuif.

Antoine runs away. We learn from the outline for the script of *Antoine et Colette*, the second chapter in the Doinel story, that he is brought back and finally released, thanks to the efforts of the sympathetic woman psychiatrist in *Les Quatre Cents Coups*. At sixteen, his parents having relinquished their authority, he works for Philips in a menial capacity, classifying and later pressing records, and spends his spare time at the lectures and concerts organized by the Jeunesses Musicales de France. In Truffaut's case, André Bazin, whom he had first got to know while trying to run a ciné-club, was responsible for getting him out of Villejuif. Again the psychiatrist helped, and again Truffaut's parents abdicated their legal rights over their son. Bazin found him a job running film shows in factories for an organization called Travail et Culture – roughly equivalent to the

W.E.A., though associated particularly with the postwar activities of Resistance veterans. Truffaut then worked as a welder, and spent his spare time at the Ciné-Club du Faubourg and increasingly at the Cinémathèque. Like Antoine, he fell violently in love, went to live in a hotel opposite the home of his beloved, and spied on her comings and goings. His love was not requited. The Bazins fulfilled the role of adoptive parents for him just as Colette's parents do for Antoine. Truffaut voluntarily enlisted in the army, went absent without leave, languished in several military prisons, and was discharged – with some help from Bazin – for 'instability of character' at the age of twenty. This is also Antoine's situation at the beginning of *Baisers Volés*. From this point on the autobiographical parallels become fewer, with more divergencies than overlaps.

Bazin gave Truffaut his break as a film critic, and from 1952 Truffaut wrote regularly for *Cahiers* and *Arts*. In 1955 he made a short film, *Une Visite*, and the next year he was assistant to Roberto Rossellini, though no films came out of this period. Bazin died in 1958, too soon to see his protégé emerge, in the Sixties, as a major director. Since he began to direct, Truffaut's life has been his work, and few facts, as opposed to anecdotes, are known about his private life. His marriage, from which he has two daughters, certainly gave him the chance to make *Les Mistons* and then *Les Quatre Cents Coups*. The extent to which his own marriage is revealed in *Domicile Conjugal* and elsewhere is a matter for conjecture. We last see Antoine Doinel, after his joy in paternity and his brief, idyll-seeking adultery, reconciled with his wife in a situation of marital compromise. Antoine is now an aspiring writer, and according to Truffaut writers' lives are not interesting; so this vein is now exhausted. Truffaut himself is now divorced.

If the autobiographical details become increasingly scattered as the Antoine Doinel cycle progresses, the psychological hints as to Truffaut's personality are even more elusive. But the following tentative hypothesis, again leaning heavily on the first two films of the cycle, may be helpful in suggesting the main lines of Truffaut's character. The danger of course lies in the temptation to equate Truffaut entirely with Antoine. The further limitations are obvious. I have interviewed Truffaut several times, and I was present during the shooting of *Domicile Conjugal*; I have also talked to several of his friends and colleagues. Without reading too much into it, if we have accepted the parallel between the factual details of Truffaut's life and that of Antoine, perhaps it is not unreasonable to assume a measure of temperamental and psychological resemblance between the two.

The evidence afforded by the first two films in the cycle about Antoine's formative years is crucial. Gilberte is pregnant and unmarried. The father is absent, and she feels guilty and rejected. She seeks to suppress these emotions by doing away with the evidence, but her abortion attempt fails and the bastard Antoine is born. She rejects him; he is suckled by a wet-nurse and fostered by his grandmother. When he is eight, his mother is forced by his grandmother's senility to take over her parental responsibility. Meanwhile Julien Doinel, who is not Antoine's father, has married Gilberte and given her and the boy his name and respectability. But to his mother Antoine is a constant reminder of the past. Her resentment leads her to treat him with hostility, more as a domestic servant and errand boy than as a son.

By the age of thirteen Antoine has accepted this lack of maternal affection without bitterness. If he once desperately needed tenderness from his mother, he certainly no longer expects it. He is in any case becoming embarrassingly aware of his mother in another role. She is virtually the only female presence in his life, and the Oedipal urges, apparently dormant for so long, now begin to assert themselves. His mother fascinates him as a sexual creature; he is intrigued by the accoutrements of her femininity – her toilet water, eyelash curlers, perfume. She casually removes her stockings, in Truffaut's words 'that silken skin more disturbing than the real one', in Antoine's presence, as if he were immune to the sight of her bare thighs. She seems curiously unaware of the effect she has on him as he grapples with the onset of puberty and the stirrings of half-understood desires. He observes her furtively as she steps over his bed in the corridor. He overhears conversations between his parents in which sexual hints and overtones, innuendoes on themes such as working overtime and payment for services rendered, puzzle and disturb him. The images of love to which he is exposed on the cinema screen or in pin-up photographs are associated with clandestine pleasure and enjoyed in secret. Then his mother, the unattainable taboo figure, suddenly shatters his illusions about her.

Monsieur Doinel has never really been an obstacle or a rival in the classic Oedipal sense to Antoine's (mental) enjoyment of his mother

Les Quatre Cents Coups: 'His mother fascinates him as a sexual creature' (Claire Maurier, Albert Rémy)

– first because he is not Antoine's father, and secondly because he is in any case a weak and complaisant husband. So Antoine has been free to indulge his private fantasies, in which he reigns supreme in his mother's affections. His discovery of her embracing another man in the Place Clichy has a traumatic effect on him. His idol – who is also the object of his 'pure', because unconsummated, desire – is sullied and tarnished, and in his state of shock this is not an image which his conscious mind can accept. When he returns to school next day and offers his mother's death as an excuse for his absence, the choice of parent to kill off is thus highly significant. His father is no threat, so Oedipal patricide is not called for. But his mother's attempt to cut Antoine off at birth is paralleled by his desire now to kill her off. And any guilt feelings about his repressed incestuous desire are thus also assuaged. It is the ideal solution for the severely wounded Antoine, and he grasps at it in desperation.

When it fails and Antoine is confronted with reality in the shape of his mother – very much alive – and his own imminent punishment, to be administered by his parents, his second solution, which proves equally temporary, is to run away. His English teacher's suggestion that 'perhaps it's all to do with his glands' may not be a particularly helpful comment on Antoine's struggle with the problems of puberty, but at least in so far as it contains a grain of truth our first impression that it is merely ludicrous is not quite the whole story. Antoine's adolescent crisis is further complicated by his mother's belated solicitude for his well-being and her simulated affection – based on her own self-interest – for her son as she takes him home after this escapade. Her concern here is simply to establish a complicity with Antoine to ensure that he does not reveal to his stepfather the existence of her lover. Her method is unsubtle bribery, as she attempts to discover common ground with Antoine by commiserating with him on his need to have secrets from his parents, or at least from one of them. She is again totally oblivious to the fact that Antoine's sexuality is awakened by her femininity, as she puts her arm round his shoulders, bathes him, dries him, embarrasses him by kissing his body and cuddling him. The final, incestuous touch is supplied by her insistence on tucking him up in the parental bed – Monsieur Doinel displaced at last; mother buying son's silence as a man might pay off a whore. Shortly after this feigned show of maternal affection, on their return from a happy family trip to the cinema, Julien shows off his wife's legs to Antoine, who later discovers him lustily squeezing her breasts, to her evident satisfaction.

Antoine's emotional weaning is brusquely completed by his mother when she visits him in the Reform School, the only other occasion in the film when he and his mother are together. She tells him of the unity which exists between Julien and herself, despite appearances to the contrary. From now on, as a result of Antoine's attitude, they will take no more interest in him; let him try manual work and earn his own living. The break is complete. Antoine's behaviour pattern when faced with a crisis remains consistent: he runs away. At the end of *Les Quatre Cents Coups* he is at last free – and utterly alone.

The other female influences in *Les Quatre Cents Coups* are relatively slight. The little girls seen at the puppet show and those locked up, for their own protection, by the porter at the Reform School are obviously too young. The possibility that Madame Bigey,

René's mother, could become a substitute mother for Antoine is ruled out by her chronic alcoholism and premature ageing. Antoine's curiosity is aroused by the three prostitutes locked up with him at the police station and by Pigalle at night with its strip shows, but he is too young to take his place in this world and, when he once waited for a young prostitute who was alleged to specialize in initiating young men, she never turned up. His transitory condition, midway between boyhood and manhood, is emphasized by the episode with Jeanne Moreau. As he is helping her look for her dog, his role is usurped by Jean-Claude Brialy, an older man. Antoine's contact with women remains on a fantasy level, at a distance.

There are hints that his future quest for a mother-substitute, and also an idealized, unattainable, goddess-type woman, could be temporarily satisfied by the psychiatrist at the Reform School, who combines sympathetic interest in Antoine with feminine provocation. We never see her, but by hearing her voice and seeing the effect she has on Antoine as she questions him about his intimate experiences, we recognize her as a *femme fatale* figure with maternal overtones, 'a Rubens who had read *The Second Sex*', as Truffaut says, who seduces Antoine verbally: 'You wouldn't like to stay for hours in this office?' But this potential relationship is not developed, and the psychiatrist's main role proves to be the purely practical one of helping to secure Antoine's eventual release.

If the maternal influence in Antoine's life is unsatisfactory, paternal authority is even more lacking. In the absence of Antoine's real father, Julien is a wholly inadequate substitute. He is a failure in all his roles – husband, lover (by implication), wage-earner, power-seeker, father – and he seeks escape and fulfilment in organizing car rallies. He is a complaisant cuckold who intermittently protests about his position but is not prepared to do anything to change it, just as he grumbles ineffectually about his office situation. Spasmodically he asserts arbitrary authority over Antoine, usually in the form of a brutal beating, but he has no chance of gaining Antoine's admiration or even his respect. The best he arouses is sympathy and a kind of male complicity, as if he needs Antoine as an ally in the campaign against Gilberte. This is best expressed in the scene where they prepare to eat together 'entre hommes' and Julien symbolically dons Gilberte's apron and cracks eggs interminably into a frying pan to Antoine's great amusement.

There are no strong paternal figures who might replace Julien in Antoine's esteem. The schoolmaster's reign of petty tyranny, based on a cynical system of arbitrary punishment, does no more than reinforce Antoine's sense of the injustice of the world; and the summary justice meted out by the Reform School supervisor is calculated to instil grudging submission rather than recognition of the motive behind the castigation. Not until he is sixteen and meets Colette's parents does Antoine find the 'family' he is looking for. They continue to exert a parental influence over him, reappearing in *Baisers Volés* in the guise of the Darbons, Christine's parents, who in *Domicile Conjugal* actually become Antoine's parents-in-law. One might trace the parallel with Truffaut's own need for male authority figures. First Bazin: 'He was the "just man" that you liked to be judged by, and a father to me. Even his reprimands were precious to me, for they were proof of an affectionate interest which I had been deprived of as a child.' Then perhaps also Rossellini, Hitchcock and Renoir, the last two in a professional capacity. The further working out of Antoine's search for mother substitutes, for example in the shape of Christine Darbon, and for ideal women, like Fabienne Tabard, will be taken up later.

This psychoanalytical sketch of the character of Antoine Doinel is of course incomplete in that it concentrates mainly on post-Freudian details at the expense of other factors, particularly environmental influences. I hope to redress the balance when I come to examine each film in detail. Meanwhile there is one more factor which must be taken into account, and that is the personality of Jean-Pierre Léaud and his influence on the shaping of the character of Antoine Doinel.

The first striking phenomenon to note is the duplication, with inversion of roles, of the Truffaut-Bazin relationship, with Léaud as the adoptive son. There is thus a sense of continuity in this disciple-tutor relationship, made more poignant by Bazin's death just after shooting began on *Les Quatre Cents Coups* and the dedication of the film to his memory. So Léaud, fourteen when Truffaut first met him following an advertisement in *France-Soir* and selected him for the film, was initially very much Truffaut's creation in his own image, the 'artist as a young man'. And the character of Antoine retains the essence of Truffaut's personality throughout the first two films of the cycle.

Then in *Baisers Volés*, and especially in *Domicile Conjugal*, the influence of Léaud becomes progressively more apparent. The character seems to escape from his creator and to take on a life of his own. Renoir talks of the same phenomenon, whereby a character gradually begins to reflect predominantly the actor playing the part rather than the director. Thus Antoine is less introverted, has more charm and a greater capacity to arouse sympathy in an audience than was originally anticipated by Truffaut — and these qualities are largely the contribution of Léaud. As he appears in *Domicile Conjugal*, Antoine is now a very composite character, a kind of shadowy amalgam of Truffaut and Léaud plus other influences, who, if he still displays all the habitual timidity and vulnerability of the Truffaut hero, has nevertheless veered significantly towards Léaud. Finally, as Truffaut acknowledges, his own influence on Léaud is only one of many.

At one time it seemed that Léaud was beginning to leave Antoine Doinel and François Truffaut behind, as he worked increasingly in a more committed cinema with directors like Godard and Glauber Rocha. But Truffaut used him in 1971 in *Les Deux Anglaises et le Continent*; and now, despite his repeated assertions that Antoine Doinel is dead, plans to resuscitate him one day in a new film (Antoine is to have a nervous attack causing him to look back over his past life, which will be shown in flashbacks from the early films; thus threequarters of the 'new' film exists already). Though we may conclude — with Delphine Seyrig, a decade after *Marienbad*, appearing as a vampire in a Dracula film called *Daughters of Darkness* — that predictions about actors' future roles are clearly fraught with hazard.

4: Les Quatre Cents Coups

However far the mature Léaud may be his own man, the adolescent Léaud in 1959 in *Les Quatre Cents Coups*, his and Truffaut's first feature, is very much moulded in the director's image. Truffaut now gives individual shape, in the person of Antoine Doinel, to his composite portrait of adolescence sketched in *Les Mistons*. The full feature length gave Truffaut scope to examine the world of the thirteen-year-old in some depth, and with the rare acuity of the adult whose memory of the same period in his own life is still raw. 'I had a fairly painful memory of my adolescence which contrasted with the regrets that others generally have for their youth ... I wanted to express this feeling that adolescence is a bad moment to get through.'

The action of the film contains very little pure invention. It is based on events which happened to Truffaut or his friends, and thus illustrates Truffaut's need in films written by him to seek authenticity by filming the real-life experiences of himself and others. His diffidence is revealed in this reluctance to rely entirely on his own creative imagination, as if the inclusion of the 'vrai' were an automatic guarantee of 'vraisemblance'. His self-confidence is further shored up by his working again with children: 'Adults inspired me with fear. Being afraid of adults, I was afraid of actors. I only felt at ease with children, with those younger than myself.' He has an instinctive affinity and sympathy with these underprivileged outsiders in the adult world.

The virtual absence of technical experiment and Truffaut's lack of interest in general theories or philosophical arguments in *Les Quatre Cents Coups*, and indeed throughout his work, result in his present position, which he describes as 'the least modern and the least intellectual of all the New Wave directors', and in his virtual abandonment by the more technique-conscious theoreticians of the New Wave. Yet as we have seen, he had never wanted to revolutionize the French cinema, merely to return to the 'good' traditions of the Thirties, represented by Vigo and particularly Renoir. Like Renoir, Truffaut uses an essentially linear narrative approach to explore the main centre of interest – the characters. And his sympathetic portrayal of people owes much to the lyrical humanism of both Renoir and the Vigo of *L'Atalante*.

As the character most often seen in close-up in *Les Quatre Cents Coups* and the focal point of the whole film, Antoine engenders a strong feeling of empathy in the audience. His central position focuses our attention on his condition and leads naturally to an attempt to analyse his behaviour. But this analysis is incomplete if it neglects to stress the environmental influences of which Antoine is a product. For the more Truffaut concentrates our attention on Antoine, the more, paradoxically, we are aware of the sociological implications of his plight. Indeed the way in which Truffaut situates his characters socially, so as to show the influence of background upon behaviour, is almost as meticulous as the detailed portraits of society produced by the author he most often quotes in his films – Honoré de Balzac. Antoine's condition could figure as a classic example of deprivation in any social worker's casebook. The step from his particular case to the general implications is an easy one, though it should be stressed that Truffaut's main aim, as outlined in several interviews, is to depict Antoine the individual rather than Antoine the symbolic spearhead of an attack on social conditions.

Truffaut's depiction of Antoine is unusually convincing on the level of verisimilitude. The authenticity of the portrait is enhanced by the quasi-documentary style of the camerawork. The restrained, unemotional treatment has the effect of inducing spontaneous sympathy in the spectator and a feeling of collective responsibility, even guilt. Antoine has not been much aware that 'Heaven lies about us in our infancy'. Rather, as 'Shades of the prison-house begin to close upon the growing boy', one would say that 'he beholds the light' or at least glimpses the sea, with its womb-like quality the symbolic goal which, once attained, should free him from his present troubles. The

36

'Ludicrously incongruous love poems about hares': pedagogic practice at Antoine's school

whole film is structured round this prison/escape theme and the illusory nature of the freedom which Antoine can achieve. He proceeds in a series of picaresque adventures from one repressive institution to the next. School, family, police station, reform school, each milieu is equally inappropriate to Antoine's problems, and the adults in each setting have neither the time nor the awareness to give him the understanding he needs.

The educational system gives Antoine his first lesson in injustice. At school they are made to copy from the board, learn by heart, recite and write formal essays. Ludicrously incongruous love poems about hares, spelled out in a pedagogic voice, are rustic irrelevancies to these city toughs, and are rightly sent up by them with a rather exaggerated series of amorous sighs, wolf whistles and Marcel Marceau-type embraces round their own necks. The teacher, Petite Feuille, is the enemy who rules by force, alertness, sadism, sixth sense, sarcasm and an arbitrary system of punishment (provided a culprit is found, it doesn't matter too much who it is). The irony is quickly pointed by a shot of the Liberty, Equality, Fraternity device above the school gateway. The teacher's reign of terror is a solution of despair arising from his own bitterness and disillusionment. The nearest he gets to encouragement of his pupils is to cuff a tousle-headed boy affectionately, a gesture with latent homosexual over-tones in this all-male society, reminiscent of the behaviour of the grotesque biology teacher in Vigo's *Zéro de Conduite*. His other hypocritical and pathetically inadequate reaction is seen in his attempt to change from his role of petty tyrant into that of a teacher 'in whom one should always confide' when Antoine has shocked him with his desperately improvised reason for absence, the 'death' of his mother.

On the one occasion when Antoine's imagination is fired − by reading Balzac's *A la Recherche de l'Absolu* − his attempt to reproduce the final paragraphs from memory for a class essay is unjustly treated as plagiarism and leads to his expulsion from the class. Bécassine, the other teacher glimpsed briefly, has a pronounced stammer, which gives him enough communication problems in his own language without the complications of trying to teach a second, English. The headmaster is simply a pacifier of parents.

Antoine's sense of the injustice of his punishment leads him to rebel, and his rebellion takes the form of escape from the confines of the system. Happiness is possible only when he is liberated from the prison of school and, following his friend René's example, he plays truant. At the fairground his sense of liberation, as he is whirled round on the rotor machine, with the camera tilting from his feet to his face, is an explosion of ecstasy. It also shows him alone at the centre of his emotion. René can only follow him so far; he watches Antoine here, just as later he will not be allowed in to visit him at the Reform School. Antoine is alone in all his major experiences.

The portrait of the adults and particularly of Antoine's parents in *Les Quatre Cents Coups* is harsher than Truffaut originally intended. He has said that during shooting, uncertain of audience reaction, he underestimated the huge amount of sympathy there would be for Antoine and needlessly overemphasized by way of contrast the unsympathetic natures of Gilberte and Julien. He tends to compensate for this in the rest of the cycle where humanity is seen through much more rose-tinted spectacles, possibly because of the influence of his co-scriptwriters Claude de Givray and Bernard Revon. In *Les Quatre Cents Coups* the relationship between Antoine and his parents is further aggravated by their cramped living conditions. Antoine's bed is jammed in the narrow corridor of the tiny flat, and from it he overhears conversations not intended for his ears in which he is referred to dispassionately as 'le gosse', more of an organizational problem than an object of affection. He is made to do the household tasks – laying the table, stoking the boiler, running errands and emptying the oozing household refuse can – as part of his normal routine, which increases the audience's sympathy for him and hostility to his parents. Domestic disputes are the norm – sometimes arising from Gilberte's scorn for Julien prompting her extra-marital activities as a working wife in every sense of the expression, often over money matters or Gilberte's failure to do the domestic chores. The only really joyful family occasion is an isolated and spontaneous mood of hilarity which they all share as they return from a trip to the cinema.

Antoine's response to this home environment is again flight. With precocious gravity he informs his parents by letter that life with them is no longer possible, and escapes to live clandestinely at René's house after spending one night dossed down in a printing works. The central theme – that freedom is inextricably linked with isolation – is again illustrated here as Antoine walks alone past shop windows,

A rare moment of happiness *en famille*; Antoine on the run; and (*opposite*) the theft of the typewriter some containing feminine underwear, and in the grey dawn steals a bottle of milk and gulps it down in front of a poster advertising skiing holidays – two aspects of a world which is a thousand miles from his own at this moment. He makes a token attempt to integrate with a society whose rules are incomprehensible to him, as he breaks the ice in the fountain in the Place de la Trinité and scoops a symbolic trickle of water over his face, before going back to school.

The world Antoine inhabits is as fascinating and squalid as Balzac's teeming Parisian underworld a century before. Here crime is the order of the day. Mauricet, the school sneak, steals from his parents; so does René; pockets are picked in the school cloakroom; everyone fiddles his business expenses. Antoine and René see crime as a means of achieving independence, and at the puppet show, in contrast to the bewitched wonderment and spontaneous emotion of the little children in the audience, they plan their first crime. The execution of it is left to Antoine, René sees to that. The influence of Hitchcock, noticeable before in the repeated close-ups of Antoine, is

The theme of imprisonment: Antoine at the police station and the reform school

seen again here in the way Truffaut shoots the theft of the typewriter, and later Antoine's abortive attempt to return it when they have been unable to pawn it at the Mont de Piété. The sequence with Antoine in close-up, seen from the point of view of the concierge and suddenly interrupted by a hand on his shoulder, generates suspense in a way reminiscent of the classroom scene when Antoine's parents appear in the doorway and are seen first by the teacher, with the camera then panning to a close-up of Antoine, petrified, before tracking back to show his parents.

Antoine's Paris is largely the Montmartre-Pigalle area centring on the Place Clichy, the Place de la Trinité, the steps of the Sacré Coeur – the same sleazy Paris of the prostitute, pimp and criminal, a Paris whose lights dazzle him as the police van takes him through it *en route* for the detention centre. His confinement in the police station for part of the night is little more than a restatement of the theme of his isolation from society. A succession of shots of Antoine seen through bars – in the police cell, caged in the 'chicken coop', in the police van and in the cell at the Reform School – powerfully establishes the imprisonment theme, and also ensures our total identification with Antoine's condition. The process, as he is stripped of all his belongings, put into drab uniform, photographed in two frozen poses which make him look like a sullen thug, is designed to produce a dehumanized object (an echo here of Hitchcock's *The Wrong Man*). And the regimentation to which he is now subjected is there to induce in him a state of mindless obedience, to create an acquiescent automaton who may then be reintegrated into society.

But it will take more than this to break Antoine. The urge to escape – symbolized in the film's title with its overtones not merely of punishment but also of wild liberty – is the strongest instinct he knows. René may well be blasé about the seas and oceans he has known; Antoine has never seen the sea and is therefore irresistibly drawn towards it. The final sequence of the film is much more than a homage to Vigo's *L'Atalante*, it is an encapsulation of the central theme of the bleakness of freedom once attained. This sequence is a landmark in the history of cinema. A continuous long take of Antoine running along roads is followed by a slow pan across the Seine estuary. Two successive pans show Antoine, still running through the undergrowth, then running in a shuffling hobble across the deserted sands. On the soundtrack the string accompaniment is

'The bleakness of freedom': the penultimate shot of *Les Quatre Cents Coups*

now slower and more jerky, giving way to *pizzicato* at the end. Antoine slows down as he reaches the sea, takes a few paces forward, stops and turns to face the camera. The image freezes as he looks back at us. Not one of his problems is solved, but the indictment of society is complete.

5: Antoine et Colette

The final cutting of the umbilical cord at the end of *Les Quatre Cents Coups* eventually leads Antoine, some three years later at the age of sixteen, to his independent, solitary status in *Antoine et Colette*. This sensitive sketch, Truffaut's contribution to the international compilation film *L'Amour à Vingt Ans* (Andrzej Wajda was another contributor), would be simply a charming, lightweight diversion if it had to stand by itself. But in the context not of the rest of the film but of the Antoine Doinel cycle as a whole this portrayal of Antoine's first fumbling contact with the opposite sex establishes him already as the diffident, vulnerable dreamer of the later films.

Predictably, after a childhood deprived of affection, Antoine's first love affair is both violent and painful. At last his vision of the ideal woman can take tangible shape; the only problem is that the dream fades away when given reality and leaves Antoine achingly unfulfilled. He now has a squalid room in the Place Clichy and works as a records classifier with Philips. His need to escape from his environment here takes a less physical form than in the previous film – he immerses himself in classical music, which provides a constant background to the film. He is attempting to remedy at least one of the inadequacies of his prematurely terminated formal education by attending all the lectures and concerts organized by the Jeunesses Musicales de France.

A flashback insert (shot for *Les Quatre Cents Coups* but not used in the final version of that film) shows Antoine and René at René's house and Monsieur Bigey's tacit connivance in Antoine's presence. This is more than Truffaut's bow to himself; it plunges the audience immediately into the emotional climate of the previous film and ensures the continuity of our sympathy for Antoine. René, always the more practical and worldly-wise, is now beginning a career in the Stock Exchange. He functions here chiefly as a sounding board for Antoine's monologues on his experiences with women. His own affair of the heart with his cousin is altogether more circumspect than Antoine's flamboyant passion, though perhaps he is less in control of his relationship than he wishes to appear, since the love letter he shows Antoine, covered in heavily lipsticked kisses, is close to the wildly romantic fantasy passions of *Les Mistons*.

Antoine succumbs to the total intoxication of first love in the Salle Pleyel, as the climax of Beethoven's 'Eroica' symphony floods over him. In a series of some forty shots Truffaut crosscuts between Antoine and Colette and the orchestra. The accelerating tempo of the music, counterpointed by the increasingly frenzied speed of the cutting, echoes Antoine's rising emotions until the final close-up of him overwhelmed by the combined force of this musical and amorous 'coup de foudre'.

A series of flashbacks, commented on by Antoine, of the three occasions when he has seen Colette, charts the love-at-a-distance phase and reveals the diffidence and timidity which are the hallmark of this typical Truffaut hero. René's advice, that with the approach work over he should now attack (again an echo of *Les Mistons* and a recurring Stendhalian theme noticeable for example in *Tirez sur le Pianiste*), ironically precedes Colette taking the initiative as she borrows Antoine's programme while he is manoeuvring for a conversational opening. Truffaut uses a commentary, spoken by an omniscient narrator, on two occasions in this film, as if the mood had not been clearly established by the visuals. On each occasion the message is ominous as far as Antoine is concerned. Colette is said to treat Antoine merely as a friend or distant cousin, and later the only advantage of Antoine's removal to the hotel opposite her home is his virtual adoption by Colette's parents rather than a newfound intimacy with the creature of his dreams.

This need to reinforce the significant moments with a verbal commentary is typical of Truffaut's reluctance to rely on the more specifically 'cinematic' ingredients at his command, and his diffidence in this respect seems a limitation here, though it contributes positively to the success of other films. In general, given a hypo-

Antoine et Colette: Antoine moves house

thetical choice between a word and an image, one feels that Truffaut's instinctive fondness for language would normally incline him towards the word. Sometimes, especially in *Jules et Jim* and *Les Deux Anglaises et le Continent* and also in the recital of books in *Fahrenheit 451*, because of his wish to preserve the beauty of the original language; sometimes, as in *L'Enfant Sauvage* and presumably here, because a commentary is also actually an economical and efficient technique. The impression in *Antoine et Colette* that the commentary is used simply on grounds of expediency and that it intrudes into the narrative flow might have been avoided if Truffaut had used it throughout as an integral part of the film.

Truffaut's sketch of Colette would, if developed, take its place in the long line of screen 'bitches' which fascinate him in the films of others and to which he has added in his own films, particularly in *La Sirène du Mississippi*. In her offhand, insensitive treatment of Antoine, Colette casually exercises her power over him until she reduces him virtually to the status of an asexual object. She requires flattery, adulation, variety; he can only offer total, possessive adoration. The chasm between them is illustrated by the sequence at the cinema where Antoine, having risen to the job of actually processing records and wishing no doubt that he was the artist responsible for the song rather than the artisan who made the recording, offers Colette his first disc. Then in a repetition of the concert hall 'coup de foudre' rhythm, Truffaut crosscuts between a Movietone newsreel of a skier in the men's slalom and Antoine and Colette in the audience. He is allowed to hold her hand (no reciprocation), caress her neck and cheek (she is as cold as stone), kiss her cheek (only a gentle rebuff) but not her lips (shades of the prostitute in *Baisers Volés*); his clumsy attempt at a passionate embrace meets with a rough rejection, as the skier crunches face-first into the snow.

Antoine's emasculation as far as Colette is concerned is completed by his progressive assimilation into her family. The mother – blonde, thirty-six at most, very friendly – and the stepfather (incidentally played by François Darbon, whose name Truffaut uses for Christine's parents in the remaining two films in the cycle) – a self-made man ('Education gets you nowhere') quipping, 'Take Victor Hugo, he denounced evil but never found the remedy' – provide the relaxed, affectionate background which Antoine needs. Colette's question, 'Where is one better off than in the bosom of one's family? Answer: anywhere else,' is true in the context of Truffaut's portrayal of the domestic scene elsewhere but emphatically untrue in this present context. More than being merely adoptive parents to Antoine, Colette's parents anticipate the generous portraits of humanity in *Baisers Volés* and *Domicile Conjugal*. As they turn their backs to the camera to watch television with Antoine, after Colette has just gone out with her current suitor (called Albert, a name used later for the lover-on-call in *Jules et Jim*), the image speaks eloquently of human solidarity and warmth, which is possibly a more than adequate consolation for the pains of unrequited passion. This sympathetic emphasis on friendship is an important feature in most Truffaut films, particularly of course in *Jules et Jim*, and after a gap of several years it is taken up again in the sequel to this sketch, *Baisers Volés*.

6: Baisers Volés

Like all the films in the Antoine Doinel cycle, *Baisers Volés* is firmly set in the world of everyday reality. The nostalgia in the film is not merely for things past, and particularly for Truffaut's own youth, but also a yearning for absolutes in a world of compromise. Antoine is not of the stuff that heroes are made, especially tragic heroes, and his inherent romanticism and search for the perfect woman are never sufficiently all-embracing to cause him great suffering, nor so inflexible that they are incapable of moderation and adjustment to the possible. The world may indeed be a shabby place, but it is Antoine's world and he is at home in it. For all his charm he is a mediocrity, inspiring in an audience not the wish to emulate him but a recognition of the ordinary man's limitations.

The same is true of the rest of the human pageant which Truffaut parades before us, with one important qualification, which is that he asks us to share his own indulgent, uncritical tolerance of humanity, warts and all; a view epitomized in the euphoric death-bed discovery of Fabienne Tabard's father that 'les gens sont formidables'. Against this background Antoine's adventures, however closely we identify with him, never evoke the extremes of agony or of ecstasy – sadness and happiness, the bitter-sweet, yes; but the gamut of human emotions over which Truffaut ranges is restricted. This framework is both the limitation and the strength of *Baisers Volés*, and of most of Truffaut's films. Even though he may incidentally touch on other themes, his instinctive subject matter is the human love affair and his strength lies in his sensitive charting of the minute fluctuations of the heart. Whenever Truffaut senses that he might be approaching the doom-laden passions of the Racinian universe, he sheers away, introducing a piece of comic business or a whimsical anecdote, for if his audience must not be bored neither must it be too disturbed. Whatever else he may be, Truffaut is an entertainer, a showman, and the succession of incidents and episodes in *Baisers Volés*, tenuously linked by the personality of Antoine, provides him with his ideal framework.

The Charles Trenet theme song (composed in 1943) with which the film begins and ends also supplies the title. The implication, that fleeting moments of happiness are all that may be snatched, recalls the fundamental pessimism of Thomas Hardy's view of happiness as 'but the occasional episode in a general drama of pain'. The mood of nostalgia, tender regret for faded happiness, is instantly established, though it will be subsumed in the general theme of ideals modified to a human scale. The relationship between the sexes tends to get polarized in Truffaut's world into the true love/lust dichotomy first expressed in *Les Mistons*. Between these poles is the twilight zone of compromise in which most of the couple relationships function, inside or outside marriage. Antoine's problems at either end of the scale, and in the middle, spring from his inability to recognize the limitations of each relationship and to channel his romanticism accordingly. His anachronistic behaviour in this respect, and his confusion of literature (via Balzac, Vigny or William Irish) and life, has a famous literary parallel in the disastrous adventures of Don Quixote, once his head has been turned by too much reading of the romances of chivalry.

Summoned from an atmosphere of earthy masculine camaraderie in the military prison where, incongruously, he has been reading Balzac's story of unconsummated love *Le Lys dans la Vallée*, Antoine overhears his sergeant-major giving a lecture on mine detection in which the parallels between military and sexual terminology (unexploded mines, like women, must be handled with care) again recall the language of *Les Mistons*. After his dishonourable discharge from the army, at the age of about twenty-one, he asserts his masculinity by rushing off, still in uniform, to the nearest prostitute. His air of being in a hurry, casually whistling to feign the confidence he does not feel and the experience he does not have, falters when it is obvious that he is not familiar with the procedure of paying on entry, and collapses entirely in the face of the extreme functionalism of the

Innocence and experience: Antoine learns the rules of the game in *Baisers Volés*

sex on offer. The prostitute refuses his aggressive kiss (never with the customers), moves away when he tries to stroke her hair ('I've just lacquered it'), and disengages herself from his attempt to stroke her breasts and remove her sweater ('I'll keep it on, I've had bronchitis'). When she prepares to wash him, Antoine's ardour is cooled, and his nerve and will fail. This clinical detachment is too far from the emotional involvement he needs and – misguidedly – expects.

Rushing downstairs, as always in moments of panic or embarrassment, he encounters a second prostitute arranging the next meeting with a regular client, and she seems to offer the affection he wants. Truffaut here uses a recurring device for indicating sexual desire – a shot of a woman's legs from the point of view of a man following her upstairs. Antoine, despite his uniform, is no longer in the army, so her quip about his being in the artillery and her liking for big guns has an ironical ring. The third episode with a prostitute, much later in the film, reveals Antoine's increased experience. He now pays the prostitute at once and does not expect her to remove all her clothes

53

or prolong the encounter. This new attitude can also be seen as an assertion of life in the face of death, sex as an antidote to neurotic despair, for this encounter immediately follows the funeral of Monsieur Henri, his colleague at the detective agency, whose Bazin-like paternal guidance is thus brusquely cut off. Antoine's reaction has been anticipated by the possibly fictitious account provided by another colleague, Paul, of his love-making with a cousin in an attic on the day of a family funeral: 'After a death making love is a way of compensating . . . one needs to prove one exists.'

This same search for identity, the need to reassure himself of his own existence, is arguably at the base of Antoine's earlier posturing in front of a mirror, repeating aloud with varying intensity his own name and the names of the two major feminine influences in his life, Fabienne Tabard and Christine Darbon. The potentially comical consequences of trying to learn a foreign language exclusively by this method of repeating aloud are developed in *Domicile Conjugal*: a clear echo of Truffaut's own frustrating experience with the sounds of the English language. Antoine's spectacular incompetence in each of his jobs – hotel receptionist, private detective, TV repair man – scarcely equips him to find fulfilment in the role-playing and professional pride which might be associated with any one of them – unlike Monsieur Henri, for instance, with his amusingly stubborn memory for details of past cases and his recommendation, based on experience, of a good restaurant for salt pork and lentils.

Nor is Antoine convincing in his ego-boosting accounts of his sexual prowess with a very tall girl ('the walls trembled'), which he relates to Paul, who is himself conducting an unsatisfying liaison with Catherine, controlled by her and marked by furtive embraces in the office washroom. Other characters, such as the vague acquaintance found rummaging in street litter bins who announces that his script is about to be accepted for television, also fall short of the images of themselves they hope to present to the world. Albert and Colette of *Antoine et Colette*, now married with a child, embarrassingly fail to make contact with Antoine during a chance encounter. Truffaut exploits all these relationships for laughter; but behind the gags one senses the sadness.

Throughout the film there is a recurring emphasis on the role of chance in life. This emphasis, as we have seen, is admirably suited to the loose episodic structure into which Truffaut can introduce at

The search for identity: Antoine alone

random casual contacts and fleeting encounters. Chance operates as an important factor at key moments in Antoine's life. It is because he happens to hear of a job as night porter that he meets Monsieur Henri, becomes a private detective and so happens to encounter Fabienne Tabard. Later a similar casual sequence leads from his chance encounter with Monsieur Darbon in a motor accident to his being the man who turns up in response to Christine's summons to repair the family television set, whence his progress into bed and then into marriage with Christine. The stranger who observes and plans and tries to shape his destiny ends up empty-handed and alone. Chance, and the extent to which life is based on chance, not choice, is central to *Baisers Volés*, as it is to *Tirez sur le Pianiste* and, fundamentally, to *La Sirène du Mississippi*.

The mask and the face, the mirage and the reality, is a motif Truffaut brings out again and again in *Baisers Volés*. The film's most subtly grotesque comic portrait is that of Monsieur Tabard, the shoe-shop proprietor. His deadpan, unconscious self-revelation in an

The vulnerable male: Monsieur Tabard (Michel Lonsdale) in his shoe shop

interview with Monsieur Blady, the head of the detective agency, together with his unawareness of the gap between his mask and his real self, is a masterpiece of sustained humour. The solemn mask proclaims that its owner has no problems, is wonderfully married to a 'superior' woman, is without racial prejudice and doesn't need friends. Underneath is revealed the vulnerable male with a strong fear of being cuckolded, no sense of humour, lecherous and with a persecution complex and fascist tendencies.

The embodiment of ideal womanhood in the shape of Fabienne Tabard (Delphine Seyrig, exuding unapproachable mystery), dream goddess and fairytale princess, is Antoine's Damascus road vision, inspiring in him awed veneration and complete enslavement. This image of beatific purity and mystic inner radiance is made for worship: 'She is not a woman, she is an apparition.' His incredulity when it appears that she has a lover (in fact himself) and is therefore corruptible is based on his certainty that 'this woman is far above such a thing'. Similarly, the homosexual's refusal to believe that his

56

'She is not a woman, she is an apparition': Delphine Seyrig as Fabienne Tabard

'friend' is now married and has a child demonstrates that Antoine is not the only dreamer who needs to idolize his beloved. Truffaut's treatment of the homosexual as a source of laughter is a good example of the film's insistence on amusement at all costs. Truffaut's intentionally comic guying of the man's petulant reaction to the truth about his lover raises an easy laugh. But this parody of the gullible lover finds an echo, as we shall see, in the declaration of permanent love by the ubiquitous stranger at the end of the film — at which point Truffaut's attitude is at least ambiguous.

The miniature love idyll between Antoine and Fabienne is highlighted by three fixing shots of the Sacré Coeur seen at different times of the day from Antoine's window in the Square d'Anvers. These shots, recalling Monet's paintings of Rouen cathedral in different lights, not only establish the chronology of events but also contribute to the emotional effect of the scenes they encompass. Antoine writes his letter of farewell to Fabienne in the best romantic tradition, referring to the 'impossibility of sentiments between them' as between Félix and Madame de Mortsauf in *Le Lys dans la Vallée*, his voice heard against a shot of the Sacré Coeur by night. The letter is sent by *pneumatique*, the Parisian system of sending express letters by underground pipeline, and its progress is followed through the sewer complex in images of unexpected beauty. Prefaced by an early morning shot of the Sacré Coeur and a municipal street water-cart, then a track to the façade of Antoine's flat, framing his window in an impressionistic, grainy-textured frozen shot, Fabienne's reply is — herself. Antoine, like Charlie in *Tirez sur le Pianiste*, is seen in bed looking like a little boy whose eyes are popping out of his head. Dismissing unconsummated love as pathetic, Fabienne with tact and delicacy reveals herself as a woman, the opposite of an apparition, exceptional and unique just as every other woman is. Antoine accepts her proposal that they spend a few hours together and then, whatever happens, never see each other again in order to preserve the exceptional quality of the relationship. Perfection in human affairs is possible only as an isolated interlude. We next see the Sacré Coeur in broad daylight, and in the shot three people whose presence menaces this fragile and transient happiness.

A more intractable type of hopeless passion is represented by the mysterious stranger in the white raincoat who appears, accompanied by his own sinister theme music, at intervals throughout the film. The way he follows Christine and spies on her is reminiscent of Antoine's behaviour in *Antoine et Colette*, which in turn, as Truffaut has admitted, was based on his own experience as a young man. A further interesting parallel, between cinema-going and voyeurism, is of course not one which Truffaut is the first to draw, but he has described how in his adolescence seeing a film was always a furtive, clandestine activity – often because he was playing truant from school or sneaking out of the house without his parents' permission. The camera as voyeur aspect is most apparent in *Baisers Volés* in the delightful sequence in Christine's house just before the end. The camera lingers in close-up along a trail of assorted television components scattered on the floor, slowly mounts the stairs (almost step by step), peeps tantalizingly into the wrong bedroom, and finally glances into the right one to reveal (gentle anti-climax) Antoine and Christine discreetly in bed. Truffaut has playfully mocked the voyeurism in us all.

The build-up to this scene is echoed in the rhythm of the final episode with the enigmatic stranger. Is the man's voyeuristic behaviour no longer a substitute for action, and does the suspense music indicate a violent climax? Not so, since Truffaut seems again to be playing, Hitchcock-style, on audience expectation. Or is he? Perhaps he could not really cope with the character, and having created him he now has to dispose of him. So he makes him deliver to Christine an incongruously solemn declaration of his eternal, 'definitive' love for her, which she predictably rejects as 'completely mad'. But the scene is doubly disturbing. Truffaut seems at this point to be injecting a note of irony, even of self-mockery, in this sidelong view of an attitude which is uncomfortably close to the aspirations of Antoine and thus of Truffaut himself. Truffaut's own nostalgia for the purity and innocence of an absolute love shows through in the scene – such a love as may be dreamed about but not attained outside the world of courtly romance.

The reality of romance is typified by the compromise affair between Antoine and Christine. Initially Christine has been for Antoine an idealized outlet for love by correspondence (cf. the anecdote on the same theme in *Jules et Jim*) until his discharge from the army. Then she takes the initiative. When they meet for the first time after his discharge, he moves as if to shake hands with her but she kisses him. She invites him to her house, provocatively invites a kiss in the

Absolute love and the reality of romance: Delphine Seyrig and (*below*) Antoine and Christine (Claude Jade) on the way to 'domicile conjugal'

cellar and seems momentarily surprised when Antoine, roused, pins her roughly against the wall, like a whore. She constantly pursues him, and in the 'dépit amoureux' scene in the park it is she who provokes their provisional break-up; although during this squabble Antoine, 'dazed by Fabienne', has proclaimed that love must be based on admiration and respect, whereas he has never felt more than friendship for Christine. Finally, she engineers his seduction, and the film ends with the implication that their life together, and their problems, are about to begin.

The human contact of the detective agency can be seen as a step in Antoine's search for a substitute family; but with Christine's parents as his future in-laws, he need look no further for the warmth and affection he enjoys at their house. And Christine herself, temporarily eclipsed by the divine power of Fabienne, is an acceptable human compromise, who offers domestic peace, comradeship and an affectionate, 'maternal' indulgence of Antoine's whims.

7: Domicile Conjugal

The final chapter in the Antoine Doinel cycle was shot in 1970, two years after *Baisers Volés* and preceded by *La Sirène du Mississippi* and *L'Enfant Sauvage*, which to some extent reiterates the themes launched in *Les Quatre Cents Coups*. There are signs in this final chapter that Truffaut has perhaps overworked this particular vein, and has not avoided the danger of repetition, with variations on what looks as though it could develop into the Jean-Pierre Léaud formula comedy.

On a first viewing the temptation is to dismiss *Domicile Conjugal* as trivial – pleasant enough, but lightweight and with no real force. Truffaut tries so hard to entertain. The gags come not singlehanded, as in *Baisers Volés*, but in battalions, with at least one gag per sequence, selected by Truffaut from the mass of tape-recorded interviews with concierges, bistrot owners, flower sellers and so on, assembled by his co-scriptwriters Claude de Givray and Bernard Revon. Life is a merry romp; people are still 'formidable', only more so. The human types who live around the courtyard where much of the action takes place (recalling the use Renoir makes of a similar setting in *Le Crime de Monsieur Lange*) are larger-than-life carica- tures whose function is to entertain. Unfortunately, they tend to enter on cue for jokey dialogue in carefully contrived 'chance' encounters. The illusion of spontaneity created in *Baisers Volés* seems to have been lost in this self-conscious manipulation of walk-on parts.

At this stage one does not expect socio-political comment from Truffaut. In *Baisers Volés*, filmed among the barricades and tear gas of the events of May 1968, he simply made fleeting allusions to the replacement of Henri Langlois as director of the Paris Cinémathèque, the demonstrations and the police violence.* So two years later it is hardly surprising that in *Domicile Conjugal* political allusions to France under Pompidou should be even more anodyne. The concierge talks about the 'dustbins of the new society'; a 'politicized' prostitute complains that her trade falls off after the middle of the month because her customers have no money left; most pointed of all is Léaud's superb timing and deadpan expression as he reads aloud from Antoine's letter to a senator thanking him for his influence in enabling him to obtain a telephone in one week 'whereas the average Frenchman has been requesting one for years'. But in general the film comes perilously close to the French situation comedy with no teeth, which Truffaut used to pan as a critic. After thus isolating, Godard-style, the 'con' in *Domicile Conjugal*, what then remains?

First, the film is a considerable success as a comedy in its own right. If a few jokes inevitably fall flat or seem contrived, most of them are right on cue, thanks usually to the inspired timing of Léaud, an instinctively 'cinematic' animal equally at home with the visual demands of mime and the verbal comedy of the anecdote. It is no gratuitous homage to Tati that shows a Monsieur Hulot character in the Métro as a train arrives: Tati has said that he sees Hulot in restaurants, at airports, everywhere but in films. So Truffaut takes him at his word and uses his best double here. In the preface to *Les Aventures d'Antoine Doinel*, which contains the scripts of the four films in the cycle, Truffaut describes how he himself was once mistaken for Léaud/Doinel by a café owner, and he seems to be claiming a similar ubiquity for the character to that of the Hulot of *Playtime*, the world of which is specifically evoked in the American sequences of *Domicile Conjugal*.

---

* Despite Truffaut's personal involvement in the battle, as co-treasurer of the committee for the defence of the Cinémathèque, he has been at pains in interviews on the subject to emphasize that this was in no way for him a generalized political commitment, but simply a way of repaying a personal debt to Langlois for his own cinematic education. Truffaut's interest was confined to ensuring that Langlois was reinstated at the Cinémathèque so that cinephiles should again be able to immerse themselves in the extra-ordinary range of films shown there, just as Truffaut and his colleagues had done in the Fifties.

Domicile Conjugal: the road to domesticity

At its best, the humour works on several levels. In one sequence in the Métro, Antoine walks in front of an advertising poster for 'Bébé Confort'. The camera remains on the poster (the audience, though not Antoine, is already aware that Christine is consulting a gynaecologist) as Antoine, expressionless as Buster Keaton, walks out of the frame for a second, then suddenly returns and looks at the poster of a smiling baby. As he tries to rush out of the station (he always runs when in a panic), he is trapped by an automatic door closing – just as he is trapped in his father-to-be situation. The implications are allowed to sink in as he stares at the baby in close-up.

During the mistaken identity interview with the boss of the American company, Monsieur Max, Antoine's toneless incantation of set phrases memorized from his linguaphone course in spoken English is cumulatively and explosively comic. His technique of using the one word he understands as a springboard for a sentence produces a wildly surreal situation unsurpassed by Ionesco. Monsieur Max: 'Do you read American newspapers?' Antoine: 'I prefer poetry to prose . . .' Monsieur Max: 'Do you have a car?' Antoine: 'I am not in a hurry, I prefer to cross the town.' Monsieur Max shows Antoine the company grounds from the window – 'It's impressive, isn't it?' Antoine: 'The birds fly high in the sky . . .' Finally Monsieur Max makes his little joke: 'The employees of my company are so pleased here, they are sad if they have to stay at home on Sundays.' (We laugh.) Antoine (serious): 'Really!' But the interest of this episode is not limited to its humour. Antoine has reached his present fluency (about Truffaut's own level) via stammered English lessons in *Les Quatre Cents Coups* and a record course in *Baisers Volés*, by which he hoped to emulate his idol, Fabienne; so there is a continuity with the other films in the cycle. Much more than this, language plays an important part in *Domicile Conjugal*, and is a recurring pre-occupation of Truffaut elsewhere, particularly in *Fahrenheit 451* and *L'Enfant Sauvage*. Without language, the implication is, there is minimal communication and therefore impoverished human relation-ships; and it is this factor which is responsible for the early collapse of Antoine's affair with Kyoko, the exotic Japanese girl (this film's version of Antoine's inscrutable woman), and his speedy return to Christine and the comfortable familiarity of their native idiom.

Comedy of character, and situation comedy of a slightly more predictable kind, arises from the cross-section of humanity in the courtyard. The range is wide, even if the subjects are sometimes a shade contrived: from a gentle smile at the eccentric Great War veteran who refuses to go out until Marshal Pétain's remains are buried at Verdun, to disbelieving laughter at the boldness of the bistrot *patron's* conspiratorial, nymphomaniac wife who attempts to seduce a stubbornly uninterested Antoine: 'You, I want you, I'll have you!' The 'strangler', as a sinister neighbour is called behind his back, provides an element of suspense, which Truffaut seems to think is a necessary ingredient in any film; though often, as here, it is superfluous, even as an indication of the volatility of public opinion, when the strangler is revealed as a television female impersonator and attitudes change from hostility to admiration. False trails leading nowhere are part of Truffaut's legacy from Hitchcock, but audience manipulation as an end in itself is a pretty barren exercise and Truffaut's use of it is unnecessary.

An altogether more intriguing phenomenon is the way Truffaut blurs the distinctions between cinema and life. In this film, apart from the Hulot character, there is the television impersonation of Delphine Seyrig, first speaking a mélange of lines from Resnais' *L'Année Dernière à Marienbad*, not all of which were spoken by her in the film, then delivering her Fabienne Tabard speech in *Baisers Volés* — about being not an apparition but a woman — and agreeing that she *is* exceptional. Christine laughs, but Antoine is disconcerted — and so are we. This merging of an actor's previous roles in films made by Truffaut and by others produces a composite screen image of the actor which is confusing enough in itself, though it may well be close to the vague public image of the star as the combined essence of all the film parts he has played. Even so, Truffaut, unlike for instance Godard, does not normally employ alienation techniques, the object of which is to distance us from the film, hinder facile identification with the character, and make us aware that we are in the cinema. On the contrary, a working principle valid for all his films has been that what is happening on the screen (with very rare exceptions, such as parts of *Tirez sur le Pianiste* and the dreamlike flashbacks in *La Mariée était en noir*) represents 'reality'. Though his definition of that reality is fairly elastic — elastic enough, for instance, to contain films within films, plugs for friends' films, copies of key scenes from films which influenced him, and a plethora of allusions in the form of verbal or visual quotations.

Access to Truffaut's inner cinematic world is obviously limited. To participate totally in the self-preening experience and the thrill of recognition when an allusion is picked up or an in-joke clicks, it is necessary to *be* Truffaut and to have experienced the thirty years' intensive exposure to films which make him the total product of the cinema that he is. Virtually the whole of his education took place at the cinema and his saturation in the medium is absolute; his claim 'Je suis cinéma' is no exaggeration. The specialist cinephile has the next best chance of penetrating this world. But what of the 'general public, who enter the cinema by chance after looking at the stills outside'? And what of Truffaut's much vaunted claim to be a non-intellectual whose films have a very wide appeal ('I work for the public of the Cinéac Saint-Lazare, for the spectator who drifts in casually to watch a bit of film before catching his train')? Well, this spectator will miss most of the references. But perhaps after all he will not be missing very much, since fortunately these references do not constitute an essential part of any Truffaut film, more a gilding of the lily; and provided the spectator is responsive to the emotional turmoil of people in love, he will be capable of grasping the essence of Truffaut.

The other major redeeming feature of *Domicile Conjugal*, apart from the comedy, is the delicacy and sensitivity with which Truffaut 'illumines the commonplace' and transforms the elements of daily life into something like a fairytale. While retaining all his habitual *pudeur*, he still achieves the frankness of an intimate confession. His method at its best is always understatement and suggestion rather than open demonstration.

The opening sequence, framing Christine's legs in close-up as the camera tracks lovingly behind her while she does her shopping and pertly corrects traders who call her 'Mademoiselle', is not just expository. It also establishes her as a sexual object now within marriage, and therefore inaccessible, except to the voyeuristic gaze of the camera (and the audience) and that of lecherous old men, such as the parking attendant who 'given the chance would not say no'. Needless to say, as usual Truffaut does not exploit the erotic possibilities; as in *Jules et Jim*, the only nakedness we shall see is that of the emotions. Whatever effect she has on other men, Christine does not exactly inspire overwhelming desire in Antoine. His peremptory peck when they meet, before rushing downstairs to the important business of dyeing carnations, reminds us that this *is* a marriage and that for Truffaut, along with La Rochefoucauld, 'There may be good marriages, but there are no delightful ones.'

Not that the nymphomaniac Ginette, with her direct frontal assault, is a threat to the couple. Antoine may lack initiative, but extreme blatancy merely intimidates him. Likewise at the brothel he is embarrassed by the overwhelming selection of whores paraded before him, and he needs to personalize the relationship with the one to whom he is eventually led, telling her that she is especially beautiful and kissing her hand as he leaves.

As the marriage deteriorates, the whole basis for its existence begins to seem insubstantial. Antoine, having missed out on the maternal tenderness phase in childhood, needs to compensate for it now; he needs to receive more affection and indulgence than he is able, or prepared, to give. By marrying Christine, a typically well-brought-up girl of the petit bourgeoisie (the sort that has always

'Bed . . . is mainly a place for talking and reading' (Claude Jade, Jean-Pierre Léaud)

attracted him, according to his ex-colleague from the television repair firm), Antoine admits to being in love not just with her but with the whole family – a kind of package deal which ensures that he will be surrounded by a comfortable, protective framework. He will have fitful moments of tenderness for Christine and will sometimes amuse and entertain her, but she will rarely be more than the audience of one in front of whom his ego flowers. Bed, for Antoine and Christine, is mainly a place for talking and reading. Antoine is initially so bashful that he tells Christine not to look while he undresses and then leaps into bed with his pyjama trousers on. Christine has not developed beyond the adolescent stage of love at a distance, and idolizes Nureyev, symbol of masculinity. Together they are like little children playing at marriage. In this context the birth of their son Alphonse is a minor miracle.

Even so, it is not as an escape from a loveless marriage that Antoine is driven to writing. His inclination (vocation would be too positive a word) has always been towards solitary self-expression, and

A minor miracle: Antoine, Christine and Alphonse

at key moments in his life he has always been alone. His solitude is especially acute when his paternal pride, as he poses for photographs of himself with the baby in the maternity ward, is deflated by Christine's telling him to leave (she too has felt alone in pregnancy). Antoine walks the streets, as in *Les Quatre Cents Coups*, unable to share his joyful news with anyone. He telephones a friend, who is not in; he meets a casual acquaintance, who profits from the occasion to borrow more money from him and whose 'merde' is the only emotional response Antoine will get that night to his declaration that he is 'fou de joie'. The loneliness sub-theme in *Domicile Conjugal* includes also the hotchpotch of characters who make fleeting contact in the courtyard or in the bistrot, and whose conversation is typified by the monologue delivered by Césarin, the bistrot owner, along well-worn tracks to an audience of one (a sewer worker) who isn't even listening and in fact drifts off while Césarin is still talking.

Antoine's explosion of passion for Kyoko, the Japanese girl who visits the American firm where he works (or rather plays) at tele-guiding model boats in a miniature harbour simulation, is little more than a restatement of the adoration of pure womanhood theme, personified by Fabienne Tabard in *Baisers Volés*. Again the initiative is taken by the woman. She gets Antoine alone with her; she drops her bracelet in the pool, thus ensuring a future rendezvous; she kisses Antoine when he is about to shake hands; she gives him the illusion of choosing how they spend the evening, but in fact she has it planned; she invites him to come again soon by writing on bits of paper folded inside wax flowers – 'Viens quand tu peux, mais peux bientôt' (lines spoken by Catherine, that other male-devouring goddess, in *Jules et Jim*). She is, according to Antoine, more exceptional even than other women because she is 'another continent' (he studies the theme in his bedtime reading), a fact which Christine fails to appreciate. But Antoine has difficulty in showing enthusiasm for Kyoko's unsmiling declaration that he is the man she would most like to commit suicide with, and the charms of exoticism begin to pale.

Already Antoine and Christine have progressed from sleeping separately to actually living separately. Their intimacy never included much sharing of unpalatable truths about each other, and Truffaut now captures this by intercutting a 'confidential' conversation between Antoine and Monique, the secretary at the office, with one between Christine and her neighbour Sylvana, the doting wife of the time-obsessed tenor whose voice periodically rings out across the courtyard. Even these 'conversations' are not much more than two people delivering monologues. Unlike Monique, who would 'marry a lamp-post if it conversed with me', Antoine reveals that he does not detest solitude, that he had been at first amused, then moved, by the hyper-politeness of the socially superior Christine, and that now he sees her as a little girl pretending to be a woman. Christine, for her part a virgin when they married, was afraid of men and also afraid of losing Antoine. Sylvana, who has previously been seen by Christine as a threat, with her 'beautiful bosom and voluptuous mouth', knows that 'all men are children' and advocates patience, for Antoine will return. Her assertion that 'life is fantastic', whereas the disillusioned Christine finds it merely 'disgusting', recalls the *Baisers Volés* theme of 'les gens sont formidables'. It also has a ring of irony in Sylvana's mouth, since on every occasion we have seen her she has been engaged in a frantic, losing race against the clock, trying to dress and

'Another continent': Antoine and the inscrutable Orient

catch up with her impatient husband, for whom, as the omniscient recluse informs us, 'time is time'.

The film's rather flimsy ending in fact takes up this theme. One year later, Antoine is back in the conjugal nest, pacing up and down and flinging Christine's bag and coat downstairs in a somewhat contrived repetition of the gestures of Sylvana's husband. Whereupon Sylvana gushingly exclaims that 'at last they love each other', which elicits from her husband three successive expressions – scepticism, wryness and mock anger – each frozen in close-up. With this, Truffaut's traditional 'ambiguous happy ending', the film closes.

Before this, though, there has been evidence of the possibility at least of survival for Antoine and Christine's relationship, in their relative honesty and tenderness at one point when they meet at the flat, drawn by their mutual consideration for Alphonse. Truffaut seems to be pointing to a limitation of his own work when Christine says pointedly about Antoine's novel, 'I don't like this idea of relating one's youth, criticizing one's parents, soiling them. A work of art can't be a settling of accounts.' Antoine's confession that he and Kyoko no longer know what to say to each other is a way of ensuring Christine's sympathetic complicity, and a preparation for her role as confidante when he telephones her three times during his interminable meal with Kyoko, complaining of his boredom, saying he wants to escape, and finding renewed tenderness in a telephone embrace with his wife. Most moving and saddening of all is Antoine's previous declaration of love and Christine's response, because it says everything about what their relationship is and what it is not:

> Antoine: You are my little sister, you are my daughter, you are my mother.
> Christine: I should also like to have been your wife.

8: Tirez sur le Pianiste

Tirez sur le Pianiste takes us back ten years to resume the chrono-logical thread interrupted by the Antoine Doinel cycle. The transi-tion is not as abrupt as it seems. Despite the fact that Truffaut's second feature is an adaptation of an American novel (*Down There* by David Goodis), it is as much a vehicle for personal expression of his recurring themes as any of the more obviously individual statements in the Doinel films. From the point of view of the film's overall tone, however, with its affectionate comic pastiche of the Hollywood B-feature and its deliberate playing on audience reaction, it can perhaps best be appreciated in the historical context of the New Wave. A helpful yardstick for comparison might be Godard's *A Bout de Souffle*, with its similar blend of melodrama, jokiness and love story and its capacity for swerving off in unexpected directions. The total effect of *Tirez sur le Pianiste* is achieved by an unlikely mixture of genres and moods which, against all the odds, results in a quirky, offbeat masterpiece ahead of its time. The essence is elusive; the effect is invigorating.

Truffaut, whose criteria for judging his own films tend to be overly influenced by their box-office performance, rates *Tirez sur le Pianiste* as a failure simply because it did not enjoy great popular success. Yet many would see it as his most idiosyncratic work and wish he had continued in the same vein. Truffaut criticizes the very qualities of 'self-indulgence' and 'self-assurance' which are the film's strengths and give it its freewheeling exuberance and bite. For once he has believed in himself and had the courage to make the film he wanted to make: not exactly without regard to audience reaction, but rather

73

with the deliberate intention of frequently disorienting and misleading his audience, Hitchcock-fashion. The film was made in the winter of 1959, in the afterglow of the dramatically unexpected success of *Les Quatre Cents Coups*, and Truffaut's change of direction, as often happens with a director's second film, was striking. The film's appeal is particularly to the sophisticated cinephile, that is to a minority audience. Truffaut was so disillusioned by the poor financial returns that he never again risked such bold experiment or allowed himself such untrammelled freedom.

Truffaut's first feature-length adaptation (Marcel Moussy collaborated on the script) from a literary source must obviously be judged as a film in its own right. But it is important in passing to compare it with the Goodis novel. Truffaut selects details of characterization, notably in the person of the pianist – Eddie in the novel, Charlie Kohler in the film* – according to his own criteria for male 'heroes'. He avoids, for instance, any mention of Charlie's hereditary violent streak in his 'wild man' past, just as he neglects much of the hard-bitten poetry of the novel. Yet he retains such aspects of the original as Charlie's sexual timidity and wish for non-involvement, perfectly captured by the inspired device of using as soundtrack at key points Charlie's 'stream of consciousness' monologue, delivered in a fast, self-mocking monotone, and gently spoofing the melodramatic commentary of many a Hollywood gangster film (as Godard did in *Alphaville* with the character of Lemmy Caution, secret agent). Given the transposition of the setting from America to France – and particularly from Harriet's Hut in downtown Philadelphia, where the novel's hero is 'a two-bit piano player without a past', to the sleazy Parisian bistrot where Charlie plays – Truffaut is remarkably faithful to the atmosphere and climate of the original, and also to the general framework and even many of the incidents. Again, the influence of the American films which Truffaut and the *Cahiers* critics saw after the war is clearly visible in this evocation of the idea of America as filtered through the B-films of the period.

After the opening close-up of the inside of a piano with the hammers pounding out the insistently rhythmic and melancholy theme tune, the first sequence plunges us at once into the atmosphere

---

* To avoid confusion I refer to him as Charlie throughout, even after the revelation of his real name in the flashback sequence.

Tirez sur le Pianiste: the influence of the Hollywood B-film (Serge Davri, Charles Aznavour)

of the gangster chase. A man is running at night down a dimly lit street, pursued by a car with dazzling headlights and screaming tyres. Suddenly he slumps to the ground – hit by the car, or perhaps riddled with bullets. Actually, he has run into a lamp-post. Our instinctive identification with the victim and our acceptance of the chase scene at face value have been mocked. This is only a spoof of the Hollywood production-line thrillers which formed Truffaut's staple film diet in post-war Paris. The action is then suspended as a complete stranger comes up, helps the man to his feet, and begins to recount his marriage – how he once thought of getting rid of his wife, but then two years after his marriage fell in love with her. A comic insert; scepticism about marriage; 'les gens sont formidables' again: familiar Truffaut attitudes all. The two men part. Then the first man, remembering he is in a gangster film, runs off again at breakneck speed as the narrative thread is resumed.

The next sequence, in the bistrot where the man seeks asylum, packs in a lot of information and concludes the exposition. The man's brother, Edouard, greets him laconically: 'Call me Charlie and wait there.' Charlie's role-playing is even more conscious than that of other Truffaut heroes. He does not want to know about the pursuing gangsters, double-crossed by a brother he has not seen for years. The affectionate reference to the Marx brothers – this brother is called Chico, there are four brothers in all – is the first of many cinematic in-jokes and allusions in the film. The introduction of the middle-aged bouncer barman, Plyne (Goodis' Harleyville Hugger, who 'has it bad for the waitress', who in her turn is 'strictly solo – she wants no part of any man'), shows his pathetic attempt to assert his author-ity – to play out *his* role – by threatening Chico, who is loudly informing the customers that his brother, Charlie, should be in a concert hall and not in this dump. Plyne is coldly deflated by Charlie, who rejects his familiarity: 'Call me *Mister* Kohler.'

Charlie thumps out mechanical rhythms at the piano, while the attitudes of the people dancing before his neutral gaze constitute an amusing microcosm of sexual behaviour. Chico attempts a cheerfully blatant pick-up ('You are very desirable. That's why I desire you') and proposes marriage. A generously endowed woman, disconcerted by her small dancing partner's frank interest in her bosom, is told not to worry because he is a doctor. And the comic patter is reinforced by the visual demonstration of the sex theme, as Clarisse, the archetypal

'Mechanical rhythms': Charlie at the piano

big-hearted prostitute, amuses herself by temporarily deserting her
role as a plaything of the customers and performing a comic dance
with a little man whom she alternately playfully entices towards her
and then physically repels, the whole performance watched by two
connoisseurs of form whose simulated world-weariness ill conceals
their own inexperience. All good, jokey fun, with Truffaut's habitual
serious undertones, until the chase is resumed with the sudden arrival
of the two gangsters, comic cut-out uglies of laughable inefficiency.
Their efforts are easily foiled by Charlie, jerked from his inner
reverie and thus involved by chance, despite his desire for isolation,
in the affairs of others.

A shot of the singer, frantically jigging up and down as he delivers
at amazing speed – in an effort to distract attention from the man-
hunt in progress – a song about Avanie and Framboise being the
teats of destiny, shows his bobbing head juxtaposed in the frame with
the faces of Victor, the constantly grinning drummer, and Charlie,
looking deadpan and gloomy. The gap between public performance and

private reality is succinctly revealed. The shot also announces the persistent melancholy of Charlie's character and situation, which tends to get lost among the film's plethora of snappy comic effects.

Plyne is revealed as simply a wreck, further down the human scrapheap than Charlie but engaged in an equally painful identity quest. In this he is hampered by limited perceptiveness and infantile illusions about the world and women, which result in a disastrous inability to make contact with anyone, including Charlie, whose soured lucidity and self-containment insulate him in an equally sterile existence. Charlie offers only mockery in return for Plyne's admiration of him and his power to attract the waitress, Léna. He rebuffs Plyne's friendship-seeking lament about being unattractive to women with the usual Truffaut flippancy that it may be gland trouble (a remark made about Antoine in *Les Quatre Cents Coups*), and takes jokingly the suggestion that his own problem is timidity; though the idea intrigues him enough for him to repeat to himself 'I am afraid' in a semi-mocking, quizzical tone which debunks Plyne, amuses the audience and suggests his vulnerability despite his smokescreen, all at the same time.

The poignant woodwind theme which Truffaut often uses for its emotional effect and especially to highlight a gentle 'true love' scene is heard now as Léna, taking the initiative, waits for Charlie, borrows money from him and asks him to see her home. The mood anticipated by the music is enhanced by the soundtrack (Charlie's inner monologue as he rehearses subtle ways of asking her for a drink, finally blurts out a direct proposal, and finds she has slipped away) and brilliantly emphasized by the camerawork: medium close-ups of the couple's head and shoulders, then a series of close-ups at waist level from the rear, stressing Charlie's tentative hand movements behind Léna's back as, fists clenched, he plans his campaign and, Julien Sorel-style, begins to count on his fingers. Truffaut's use here of the camera's capacity to create a mood, in this case humour, prefigures a similar example in *Baisers Volés*. We see a rear view of a woman's head in close-up, then a shot of her head and shoulders, then the camera pulls back to a medium long-shot of the woman with Antoine walking beside her – revealing what it has previously concealed, not merely that she is not alone but that she is taller than Antoine by at least a head. The significance of Antoine's earlier interest in special techniques for very tall girls becomes clear.

79

'The persistent melancholy of Charlie's character and situation' (Charles Aznavour)

Charlie's wry acceptance of the comic anti-climax of his man-oeuvres – 'Perhaps it was better that way' – indicates a man more accustomed to the consolations of stoical resignation than confident of his sexual prowess. The film, not for the first time, then swerves off in an unexpected direction as Charlie switches off the emotional intensity which exposes his vulnerability and enjoys a relaxed, uncomplicated, quipping sexual encounter with his neighbour Clarisse, the prostitute, in which audience involvement is again deliberately shattered by a distancing device. Truffaut mildly upbraids the arbitrary prudery of the censor, and also reminds us that we are in the cinema, as Charlie covers Clarisse's breasts with a sheet and says, 'At the cinema it's always like that.'

The reappearance of the gangsters (Ernest and Momo) next morning, heralded by a burst of melodramatic suspense music, points up again their role as comic characters, as Fido, Charlie's younger brother, bombs their car windscreen from on high with a carton of milk – another example of the consciously incongruous interpolation of gratuitous humour into an otherwise plausible love story, and typical of the film's abrupt switches of tone.

The ensuing abortive abduction of Charlie, then Léna, by the crooks, with Ernest twirling his revolver and trying to act tough (he has seen too many gangster films), offers scope for another burlesque spoof on the theme of sex. First a split-screen triple iris shot shows Plyne in three consecutive stages of betraying Charlie and Léna to the crooks, another Truffaut homage to the silent screen and in particular to Abel Gance. Then, in a pastiche of standard demonstrations of twisted criminal motivation, Momo reveals his life's quest for revenge on all women because one of them inadvertently caused the death of his father, knocked down by a car as he stared at her in the street. The sexual frenzy into which Ernest and Momo work themselves merely by talking about women as sexual objects who 'only want one thing, but expect to be spoken to as well' is temporarily interrupted by Charlie, quoting a familiar Truffaut comic maxim (used also in *La Mariée était en noir*): 'When you've seen one, you've seen them all.' Their obsession with women's clothing designed to attract men, particularly underwear and stockings, verges on fetishism, and establishes these gangsters firmly in the mainstream tradition of the Truffaut male victim.

Léna and Charlie escape, and his awareness of the danger of

falling – metaphorically as well as literally – if he looks at her legs as she precedes him upstairs to her room provides the run-in to the extended flashback sequence introduced by Léna's 'Formerly it was different'. The idyll of Charlie and his wife Thérésa in bed together is disturbed by the superimposition of an iris shot of the evil impresario Lars Schmeel; the shot, interposed between the couple, is soon faded out, but it leaves an impression of menace, like a fairytale ogre. Three shots, in progressively increasing close-up (and accompanied by a disorienting long-shot), of Charlie's finger nervously approaching the bell-push at Schmeel's door illustrate what Schmeel calls his 'illness' of timidity. The impresario later tries to eliminate this flaw in his protégé's public image by subjecting him to a course in personality projection, at the end of which Charlie resembles the required posturing stereotype (foreshadowing Antoine's mouthing of disconnected English phrases in *Domicile Conjugal*), though his real identity remains resolutely enigmatic. His career as an international pianist, pounding out the classics in the world's concert halls, produces in him both total egocentricity and at the same time doubt about his talent, and puts intolerable strain on his marriage. A sad near-embrace at the end of one sequence fades out, suggesting perhaps that the couple are doomed not to complete it. And when Thérésa's burden of guilt drives her to talk to Charlie, it is too late.

Thérésa's confession is prefaced by an ominous silence on the soundtrack. The camera crosscuts between husband and wife, then pans from face to face as she spells out the details of the love or lust dilemma involved in her sacrifice of herself to Schmeel in furtherance of Charlie's career. Charlie's tortured inner monologue reflects his own dilemma: his realization of the need to go to Thérésa and comfort her and his inability to do so. He walks out, hesitates, runs back; but the message implied in the increasingly urgent tension of the music is confirmed as the camera seems to rush past him into the room and on to the balcony, and plunges giddily down to reveal Thérésa's body on the pavement below – followed, as in *Les Mistons*, by a shot of newspaper headlines announcing the tragedy. Léna's voice then takes the narrative up to the present, and the image fades from a poster of Edouard Saroyan, concert pianist, to a succession of superimposed embraces between Léna and Charlie in bed, whose tenderness, heightened by the death scene and its accompanying sense of loss, is also reminiscent of *Les Mistons*.

Isolation: Charlie and Thérésa (Nicole Berger)

But even at this time of burgeoning love, the danger signs are there to remind us that in Truffaut's world happiness is transient. Léna takes over Charlie, organizing him into going out to buy her a pair of stockings (the same fate befalls Pierre in *La Peau Douce*) and trying to resuscitate his sense of identity by telling him to resume his career and his real name. She counters the nihilism of his 'Pourquoi?' with the pragmatism of her 'Pour qui?', but realistically asks him to have the courage to tell her when he no longer loves her. Then the comic kidnapping (comic in action, but with serious consequences) of Fido by the gangsters, and their naïve attempts, like little boys, to impress him with their musical cigarette lighters, new snorkel pens, alligator belts and other toys, allows Truffaut a moment of joyfully gratuitous farce, unthinkable in any other film, as one of the gangsters swears on the head of his mother and an iris insert shows a little old lady keeling over stricken, legs in the air.

Typically, the climax of the film — the confrontation between Plyne, Charlie and Léna — is placed within this comic sequence.

Intervention: Charlie tackles Plyne

Charlie's solitude is threatened, despite Léna's view that 'even when he's with somebody he is alone'. He tries his usual remedy of immersing himself in his music as Léna demolishes Plyne and his pretensions to masculinity. Charlie muses, 'Even now, when she's calling him names, he can't take his eyes off her. She's overdoing it, but what can I tell her? That Plyne isn't as bad as she paints him? He's a poor slob who hoped to be somebody and didn't make it.' Forced to intervene to save Léna, Charlie is exposed to the full violence of Plyne's anger and sudden disillusionment that this woman, his idol, has been 'sullied' and that she no longer conforms to his ideal. 'Woman is pure, delicate, fragile; woman is supreme, magical,' he informs Charlie, gripping him tightly round the throat in a last desperate effort to assert his masculinity, and refusing Charlie's peace offer (in what might almost be an alternative ending to *Baisers Volés*, with Plyne as the stranger and Charlie as Antoine). Charlie, on the point of choking to death, finds his discarded knife and, as in Hitchcock's *Dial M for Murder*, stabs Plyne, aiming for his arm but

'At last, after many adventures . . .': Charlie and Léna (Marie Dubois) on the run

accidentally killing him – the culmination of the note of fatalism which runs through the film. Plyne's concept of the purity of woman, though expressed in this incongruous context, is in the best tradition of declarations by dying gangsters; and also of Truffaut's misunderstood heroes.

'At last, after many adventures' (for this is a kind of fairy story), including Charlie's rescue by Léna and their escape by car, the setting changes from the lights of the city to the blinding snow of the Alps. During the journey a singer on the car radio has proclaimed, 'When I don't love you any more, I'll wear my cap,' a somewhat unsubtle touch to remind us that this *may* be a fairy story but that it is also set in a world where love ends. Charlie, 'despite himself, despite herself', sends Léna away and joins his brothers, Richard and Chico, in their hideout – actually the parental home, from which the parents have been banished.

The final gun battle with the gangsters, prefaced by a combination of the woodwind theme and the gangsters' own suspense music followed by an ominous silence, and by Léna's return to take Charlie back, epitomizes the disturbing clash of tones which has characterized the film. First, comedy – the ease with which Fido escapes from the crooks as they slip on the ice; then burlesque of the gangster film's traditional finale – gun butts shatter windows, one of the gangsters twirls his gun again, but it still looks like a toy gun. We have been manipulated into identifying with Charlie and Léna. We have been willing a happy ending, ignoring the carefully planted omens of tragedy – the song, the suspense music, the gun. The cross-cutting between Léna, Charlie and the gangsters has given us the scent of danger. But the continuing aura of comedy surrounding the gangsters has cushioned us in our expectation that the situation cannot be unhappily resolved. Then suddenly Léna is hit by a bullet, and in an agonizingly prolonged shot her body slides down the slope, insistently proclaiming the reality, and the finality, of this moment. A briefly frozen close-up of her face confirms that Charlie need not have bothered to run frantically to her. Another Truffaut idyll is over, destroyed by chance.

Charlie returns to his piano in the bar. He pounds out the haunting theme, and his bleak, mournful stare as the intensity of the music increases gives way to the opening shot of the piano hammers. The circle is complete. There is a new waitress in the bar; but Charlie's solitude is unassailable and his nihilism intact. The attractive possibility that the film might at any moment lurch in a new direction has been preserved until the end. This capacity to surprise (and mislead) the audience is what distinguishes this from every other Truffaut film. True, anything might *happen* in a loose, episodic structure such as that of *Baisers Volés*. But it is the unexpected switching of *moods* which gives *Tirez sur le Pianiste* its particular, elusive quality.

9: Jules et Jim

Tirez sur le Pianiste is the kind of film Truffaut might have gone on making if he had chosen to risk all on working out his talent for manipulating genres and moods – allusions to French cinema, echoes of America and Hollywood B-film clichés – into excitingly fresh permutations in French settings. Godard went on to do something like this. But *Tirez sur le Pianiste* is Truffaut's only contribution to this early Sixties, characteristically New Wave style of film-making; and his three other films based on American sources have little of the same exuberant experimentation. Yet if *Tirez sur le Pianiste* is the key testament to Truffaut's American inclinations, his next film is an even greater achievement in the mainstream of what might be termed the French lyrical tradition.

A hymn to total freedom in love and a lament for the impossibility of achieving it, *Jules et Jim* is Truffaut's third feature; which, by his own criteria, makes it his first 'definitive' film and the beginning of his mature work. Despite the potentially scandalous nature of the subject (even in 1961) – two men and a woman sharing life and love over a period of twenty years – Truffaut's film successfully reproduces the essential purity of the source novel, a first work by Henri-Pierre Roché, written in 1953 when the author was seventy-four.

Almost the whole of the novel is there, but with incidents rearranged and some different emphases, notably in connection with the role of Catherine, which is a composite portrait combining predominantly the personality of the novel's Kathe with the qualities of many of the other women who appear in the first part of the book.

The spirit and tone of the original, particularly its adult fairytale quality, are miraculously preserved. The actual text figures either as dialogue – occasionally transposed to different speakers or situations – or as part of the ubiquitous commentary, spoken unobtrusively but tellingly as a poetic, ironic accompaniment to the film. Truffaut has made the masculine friendship aspect secondary to the central emphasis on the dominance of Catherine, and to this extent the title is more appropriate to the novel than to the film. The failure of the heterosexual couple is the major theme of the film, together with the corollary that all other solutions, including the *ménage à trois*, are equally doomed.

In both the book and the film it is the passionate pursuit of happiness and the satisfaction of their transient desires which provide the characters with their reasons for living. In their preoccupation with personal happiness they are representative of the bohemian intellectuals and free-thinkers of the café society of the period between 1912 and the early 1930s. The ravages of the First World War and later the public book-burning by the Nazis are background episodes which temporarily interrupt but do not divert them from the dilettante activities and whimsical humour of their own lives.

The fairytale opening commentary, quickly spoken in a neutral tone, describes how in pre-war Paris a friendship blossomed between the small, fair-haired Jules from 'somewhere in Central Europe' and the tall, thin Frenchman, Jim. They are soon inseparable, sharing a love of language and literature and a relative indifference towards money. 'So they talked easily, each finding in the other the best listener of his life.' The first major difference between them is in their experience with women. 'There were no women in Jules' life in Paris, and he wanted one. In Jim's life there were several.' Jim introduces his friend to a number of women, with whom Jules is 'a little bit in love for a week' (thus telescoping incidentally several early chapters of the novel). Finally, 'against Jim's advice, Jules turns to the professionals ... but without finding satisfaction there.' The whole of the exposition has been a series of rapid, silent scenes showing the two men alone or with women, counterpointed by the affectionate commentary, like a story being read aloud.

A gentle dig at anarchists who can't spell serves as a pretext to introduce Thérèse, who picks up any man prepared to offer her a bed for the night. She is the embodiment of existential freedom. Her allegiance is to herself and to the mood of the moment, captured perfectly by her giddy imitation of a steam engine, with the camera panning after her in close-up as she puffs round the room with smoke pouring from the wrong end of the lighted cigarette in her mouth, and the music zooming along in harmony. The same routine serves later to attract another man, and Jules, guilty of neglecting her because he is immersed in conversation with Jim, ruefully declares that he wasn't in love with her: 'For me she was my young mother and my attentive daughter both at the same time.' Shades of Antoine Doinel, and the first hint of Jules' vulnerability and gentleness, as well as a foretaste of the future havoc to be wrought by a more imperiously demanding woman.

Jim meanwhile has been conducting his own experiment in carefully circumscribed freedom with Gilberte. His jealous guarding of this freedom, on the grounds that living together for any length of time would make their relationship indistinguishable from marriage, illustrates *his* need rather than hers, and in this respect sharply differentiates him from Jules. Individual freedom and happiness is again limited by rules in a gently amusing incident later in the café. Jules sketches on a round table-top the face of a woman he has loved. 'Jim wanted to buy the table,' the commentary tells us, 'but it was not possible – the proprietor would only sell all the twelve tables together.' But the atmosphere of the fairytale in which everything is possible soon takes over again. The two friends are captivated by a lantern slide of an ancient statue – a calmly smiling woman's face. They resolve to go and see it together and set off immediately for an island in the Adriatic, where they are struck dumb by the statue's beauty. The contrast here between the transience of human affairs and the permanence of art recalls some lines in Keats' 'Ode on a Grecian Urn' ('Thou, silent form, dost tease us out of thought/As doth eternity ... Thou shalt remain, in midst of other woe/Than ours ...'). 'Had they ever met that smile before? Never. What would they do if they met it one day? They would follow it.' Thus begins their worship of the goddess by whom, according to the traditions of classical mythology, they will be ultimately and inexorably destroyed.

A series of close-ups of the eyes, mouth, nose, chin and forehead of Catherine, whose smile recalls that of the statue, heralds the entrance of this personification of the deity, while the subsequent

Jules et Jim: 'Thomas always wins' (Jeanne Moreau, Henri Serre, Oskar Werner)

narrowing of the screen to frame her and Jules radiating happiness together indicates the designation of her first victim. Jules' suffering begins as he first dimly perceives the threat posed by Catherine to their idyllic masculine friendship, and the spectre of rivalry between them in his 'Not this one, Jim, eh?' Later, the success of the masculine disguise by which Catherine becomes 'Thomas' moves them 'as if by a symbol, which they did not understand'. Significantly, Thomas always wins, even if, as in the race between the three of them, by cheating a little. Her extremism may be the result of her mixed aristocratic and peasant parentage. It is her decision that the three of them should leave for the seaside; and their departure is prefaced by her ceremonial burning of letters from past lovers, which almost leads to her accidental self-immolation – another hint of mortality. Her passionate attachment to vitriol as a weapon to throw in men's lying eyes is an unhappy omen for any man who dares to spurn her.

The dazzling Mediterranean light, in the shot of them all peering at

Triangles: the transient happiness of a golden moment

the dawn from separate windows of their white house by the sea, reflects the optimism of this golden moment. But implicit in this mood is an awareness of the fragility of their happiness and the impermanence of people dwarfed by the permanence of nature and the eternities. So in a wood near the shore, to the accompaniment of the joyful strings and woodwind theme, they search for 'the last traces of civilization', symbolized by odd pieces of junk, remnants of the old order from which they are trying to escape. The camera, panning across the treetops from Jim's vantage point, reinforces the possibility of happiness in a retreat to nature, but then we come down to earth again with Jim's warning to Jules that Catherine within the bounds of marriage will never be happy on this earth: 'She is an apparition for all to appreciate perhaps, but not a woman for any one man' (a view which reflects Antoine's image of Fabienne in *Baisers Volés*). But this does not preclude the possibility of bursts of happiness, expressed most typically when the three swoop along on bicycles on a winding road, sometimes apart, sometimes side by

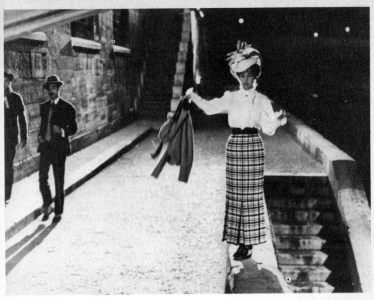

Catherine centre-stage: 'She wants to be free. She invents her life, every moment.'

side, Catherine often speeding ahead, in a visual anticipation of the permutations of their future fluctuating relationship.

Catherine's gigantic ego is happy only at the centre of things. When she is neglected, she draws attention to herself again by slapping Jules' face hard. They laugh, after an uneasy pause; and Catherine, centre stage again, is seen in a series of close-ups, each momentarily frozen, illustrating the gamut of emotions through which she has passed. Back in Paris again, Catherine's identification with the heroine of the play they have just seen ('She wants to be free. She invents her life, every moment') isolates her from the two men, who become absorbed in their own discussion. Here Truffaut puts one of his favourite comic lines into Catherine's mouth ('Men only think of one thing'), and Jules caps it with a jesting, 'Exactly, Madame, we men only ever think about one thing – and you encourage us.' Catherine's characteristic response is a melodramatic jump into the Seine, accompanied by increasingly sinister music, which frightens and silences him (with reason, as the film's penultimate sequence makes clear). The whole sequence is shot at night, reflecting the despondency of the mood at this point.

One of the key factors in the film's success, which one begins to appreciate about this point, is the quality of the performances, and particularly that of Jeanne Moreau. Truffaut's frequent tributes in interviews to her exceptional professionalism have been echoed by other directors. His claim that she is the only woman known to him who combines the 'masculine' virtues of camaraderie and strength with totally captivating feminine charm seems an understatement in the context of this film. The part is so much the actress, and vice versa, that it seems inconceivable that any other actress could have played it. Moreau outshines both Oskar Werner (Jules) and Henri Serre (Jim), and that is no fault of their fine, sympathetic performances.

Catherine misses a rendezvous with Jim in the café (she has, of course, little sense of time and less of obligation), and this gives Truffaut the opportunity to introduce one of his stock types – 'I never make jokes ... moreover I have no sense of humour' – anticipating the roles (played by Michel Lonsdale) of Monsieur Tabard in *Baisers Volés* and the sententious politician Morane in *La Mariée était en noir*. Jules announces that he is to marry Catherine, and the mood of merriment as he boisterously bellows out the 'Marseillaise' in an increasingly strong Austrian accent gives way to pathos as the image dissolves first to a poster announcing general mobilization, then to actual newsreel footage of the Great War (some of it stretched to fit the Scope frame, and so incidentally conveying an impression of war as grotesque). Personal concerns, however, remain uppermost. Jules writes passionately to Catherine from the trenches, and each man is afraid of accidentally killing the other. Then, 'Jules' country had lost the war, Jim's had won it. But the real victory was that they were alive – both of them ...'

When the trio meet after the war in the chalet on the Rhine where Jules and Catherine are living, Jim's feelings for Catherine can only be channelled through her little daughter Sabine, with whom on one occasion he rolls over and over in the grass. Sabine already imitates her mother's intonations and gestures, a *femme fatale* in embryo. Throughout the film the passage of time is reflected only in externals – a chronological procession of Picassos, Catherine's clothes, and near the end her wearing of spectacles – but the characters do not age physically and their emotional turmoil does not diminish with time. The sense of timelessness, and also the evanescence of time, is never far from the centre of *Jules et Jim*.

Jim's self-contained independence as a roving freelance journalist, 'un curieux' who can live anywhere, gives him a freedom limited only by the need to meet copy deadlines. Jules, as a biologist writer, gradually retreats into monastic seclusion, rejected by Catherine as a husband. 'I am not the man she needs, and she is not the kind of woman to put up with it.' His qualities of 'generosity, innocence, vulnerability and indulgence' (anticipating Louis in *La Sirène du Mississippi*), which in Catherine's words once dazzled and conquered her and set him apart from other men, are now tolerable to her only in doses prescribed by her, and interspersed with her absences with other lovers. Jules' plight is paralleled by the anecdote of the young gunner deflowered by correspondence, his successful wooing of the girl he wrote to from the trenches, culminating in his passionate declaration, 'Your breasts are the only bombs I know,' followed by his death in hospital on the eve of the armistice.

The rest of the film is haunted by Catherine's theme song about the whirlwind of life in which a couple are flung together, then apart, in an endlessly repeated cycle until finally they embrace for ever. Jules' altruistic self-effacement ('If you love her, stop thinking of me as an obstacle') is the prelude to the first real embrace between Jim and Catherine, seen – as in *Les Mistons* – in profile, with Jim reverently touching Catherine's forehead, nose and mouth as gently as the camera which caressed these same features of the goddess on her first appearance. 'Their first kiss lasted the rest of the night. When Jim got up, he was enslaved. Other women no longer existed for him.'

Yet Catherine's expression – 'full of curiosity and an extraordinary jubilation' – is not incompatible with her view that 'one is never completely in love for more than a moment'. Once Jim has become a fixture in the chalet, she is able to undertake the seduction of Jules in the same spirit of scientific curiosity. Jim's understanding of her attitude (as he later tells Gilberte, 'Once Catherine wants to do something, so long as she thinks that it won't hurt anyone else – she can be mistaken of course – she does it, for her own enjoyment and to learn something from it. That way she hopes to become wise') does not preclude his jealousy, captured visually by a crane shot from outside the chalet looking in first at Jim on the ground floor, zooming

'An endlessly repeated cycle': Catherine, Jules and Jim at the Rhine chalet

up to Jules and Catherine above romping on the bed, then back to Jim pacing up and down.

Recalled briefly to Paris by his newspaper, Jim encounters the unstoppable Thérèse, who breathlessly and hilariously recounts her whirlwind romantic exploits, in which her own ego has been the constant driving force. A contrasting aspect of sexuality is provided by the silent Denise, introduced to Jim by her 'owner' as 'a beautiful object ... sex in its pure state'. Having postponed his return to Catherine, whom he is to marry, because he wants to avoid hurting Gilberte, Jim finds when he does finally return that Catherine, true to her eye for an eye philosophy, is otherwise engaged. Jules and Jim are equalized as courtiers whose role is to pay homage to their (absent) queen.

Catherine unexpectedly returns, and Jim and she spend a night of trembling chastity. Another idyllic period begins. An aerial shot of the chalet and surrounding woods, taken from a helicopter, is echoed in the soaring music: 'The promised land was in sight.' Then, as the camera pulls away from the chalet, 'The promised land suddenly retreated.' Jim and Catherine's inability to produce children drives her into Jules' paternal embrace, and Jim returns to Paris after one last pitiful hotel encounter with Catherine, when 'they took each other once more, without knowing why, perhaps as a kind of full stop. It was like a burial, or as if they were already dead.' (In general, the chance of happiness in *Jules et Jim* always seems most likely in an outdoor setting – on the beach, in the meadows and forests. It tends to recede in the more confining interiors – the chalet, the hotel room, the house near Paris: an observation pinpointed by the film's strongly contrasted black and white photography.) Another aerial view of woodland, with Catherine's face superimposed on it, hints tantalizingly at the possibility of happiness offered by Catherine's news of her pregnancy. As Jim, finally convinced after a frustrating exchange of letters, prepares to respond to Catherine's summons, 'Viens quand tu peux, mais peux bientôt' (Roché's formula, used also, as we have seen, by Kyoko in *Domicile Conjugal*), the child dies in the womb and with it all further hope. 'Thus between the two of them they had created nothing.'

In an atmosphere of gathering gloom (nature again echoing emotion), a chance meeting between Jules and Jim leads to a car drive with Catherine, during which she still plays out her former role by abandoning the two men in favour of a night with Albert, one of her earlier lovers and a shadowy presence in the second half of the film. Jim's resistance to Catherine's last impassioned plea for love, and his lucid account of the reasons for the failure of their relationship ('Like you, I think that, in love, the couple is not ideal ... You wanted to construct something better, refusing hypocrisy and resignation. You wanted to invent love from the beginning ... but pioneers should be humble, without egoism'), is too much for Catherine. Truffaut's melodramatic treatment of her immediate attempt to shoot Jim is one of the few jarring moments in the film.

Jim's respite is shortlived. A few months later, in full view of Jules, Catherine's triumph is complete. In a repeat performance of her leap into the Seine, the rhythm of the editing equally fast, she is smiling inscrutably (the statue again) as with Jim beside her she drives her car over a ruined bridge into the water. Her last existential choice is made. Stark close-ups of coffins consumed by flames in the crematorium, and of grinding machinery and levers, echo the earlier

'In an atmosphere of gathering gloom': Jim and Catherine together for the last time

shots of dials and gear levers in Catherine's car, and emphasize the astonishingly swift and inevitable reduction of people to ashes. 'They left nothing behind them,' is the commentary's epitaph.

'Catherine had sown chaos in Jules' life until he was sick of it. A feeling of relief swept over him. His friendship with Jim had no equivalent in love.' The rules of society thwart Jules' wish to mingle the ashes and scatter them to the wind from the top of a hill ... 'It was not allowed.' Alone at the end, he walks downhill accompanied by Catherine's voice on the soundtrack singing about the whirlwind of life.

Existential choice: Catherine on her way to Albert; Jules with the ashes

10: La Peau Douce

At first sight it may seem surprising that Truffaut should have chosen to elaborate on the triangle theme so soon after his apparently exhaustive treatment of it in *Jules et Jim* (though in fact two years separate the films, with the *Antoine et Colette* sketch intervening). Perhaps it was the possibility of introducing very different emphases within the same overall triangular framework that induced him to make another variation on the theme. The *Jules et Jim* triangle had a strong woman at the apex and two men at the base, the whole trio being linked by friendship. *La Peau Douce* has a weak man at the apex and at the base two women who never meet; so the relationships in the film are always based on the couple – Pierre and wife, or Pierre and mistress. What is distinctive in this film about the cinematically hackneyed subject of adultery is the treatment, the style and the tone which Truffaut brings to it. His originality in *La Peau Douce* lies in his extraordinary capacity to combine severely restrained, impartial observation of his characters with a real sympathy and sensitivity to their problems. His tolerance, embracing Renoir's view that everyone always has his reasons, implies also a refusal to judge. Truffaut's concern with detailed but neutral observation discourages identification with any one character and, as in the Antoine Doinel cycle, prompts a feeling of sympathy tinged with sadness for their not uncommon circumstances.

In contrast with *Jules et Jim* there is very little of the fairytale about the unpoetical realism of *La Peau Douce*, and no nostalgic period charm to be exploited in the strictly contemporary settings – Paris, Lisbon, Rheims and Orly airport. Truffaut's original script, written in collaboration with Jean-Louis Richard, consists largely of everyday dialogue of an intentional banality. The role of language here is mainly to conceal emotion rather than to convey it. Inner passions and tensions are portrayed visually: the close-up, over which the opening credits are superimposed, of the clasping and unclasping of two hands – a woman's and a man's wearing a wedding ring – is eloquent of the film's general emphasis on impermanence and infidelity. Similarly the anxieties and pressures which weigh on Pierre Lachenay throughout the film are clearly indicated in the first sequence, which shows him emerging at speed from the Métro, looking for a taxi, forced to wait until the lights change before crossing a road, hurrying out of the lift, fumbling for the keys to his flat and finally being forced to ring for his wife Franca to let him in. From the outset Pierre hardly stops moving.

The reason for his haste – his plane for Lisbon, where he is to lecture on Balzac, leaves in forty minutes – is now spelled out, and the tension created by this piece of information (how well Truffaut has learned from Hitchcock) is increased by the staccato rhythm of the sequence showing his journey to the airport. The urgent acceleration of the music contributes to the tension as a general shot of a Mercedes pulling away, driven by Pierre's friend Michel, is followed by split-second jump cuts showing it moving at high speed. The journey is punctuated by images of urgency: close-ups of Michel's hands on the wheel; a road sign marked danger; close-up of a gear change, of Michel's hand on the horn as he overtakes, of the windscreen, of the dashboard; then an even sharper sequence of cuts from Michel's hand to his foot on the accelerator and to the windscreen wipers; then Orly airport seen through the windscreen, and finally the race to board the plane, and the sequence ends with a shot of the plane above the clouds as it begins its descent over Lisbon. An extended metaphor, then, not just of the pace and frenzy of modern living in general but illustrating the stresses among which this individual man lives.

Pierre's first glimpse of the 'soft skin' of the air hostess, Nicole, comes after they have exchanged glances in the aircraft: he stares with almost fetishist fascination at her feet, visible under the curtain as she changes her shoes. He then obliges the press photographers at the airport by posing with Nicole, and slots with accustomed ease into his public role of visiting lecturer, television celebrity, inter-

national man of letters and authority on Balzac (an inevitable choice of author for Truffaut). A link between Pierre and Charlie Kohler in *Tirez sur le Pianiste* is provided by the contrast between the suavity and confidence he displays as a public personality and the timidity and uncertainty against which his role-playing can protect him only in impersonal situations – revealed in the sequence showing him and Nicole in the hotel lift. Mounting desire, suppressed, results only in verbal impotence in this most typical Truffaut male. He needs Nicole's unsubtle ploy of dropping her room key to galvanize him into action. Even then he only gazes after her receding figure, and particularly her feet again, as she walks to her room; then he descends in the lift to his own floor and the shoe motif (homage to Buñuel?) is resumed with a rear tracking shot along the corridor of shoes outside the doors, indicating that some rooms are occupied by couples, some by a single person.

In the haven of his own room, with all the lights off, he hesitantly summons the courage to telephone Nicole, stammers an excuse for his impoliteness earlier in the lift, finally (again like Charlie Kohler) blurts out a direct invitation for a drink in the hotel bar – without realizing it is already 1.15 a.m. – and after more politenesses gloomily hangs up. Suddenly his phone rings: Pierre rushes to pick it up, Nicole suggests a rendezvous for the following day – Pierre cannot believe his ears. For the only time in the film he is blissfully happy; as the music swells to a climax, he switches on every possible light and flings himself fully-clothed on to his bed.

The next night Pierre's enthusiasm and confidence as he narrates the life of Balzac to a fascinated Nicole into the early hours of the morning seem to overflow into his relatively positive approach to her seduction, though a second lift sequence almost intimidates him again. Their first tender kiss in Nicole's darkened room, with the two faces in profile and Pierre's finger caressing her features, is Truffaut's familiar designation of a love relationship. Though despite this gentleness, and his usual discreet early fade-out, Truffaut does not entirely dispel the vague sense of disquiet prompted by the sight of a fumbling, diffident, shifty-eyed, middle-aged man about to become the lover of an attractive woman half his age. The seeds of future disaster are already sown in the audience's mind.

Later, it is characteristically left to Nicole to ensure that the relationship continues by giving Pierre her telephone number. The

101

La Peau Douce: stress (Jean Desailly as Pierre)

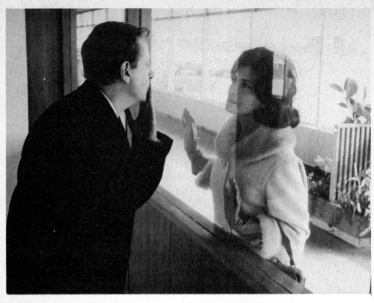

Pierre and Franca (Nelly Benedetti), symbolically separated . . .

first shot of Pierre's reunion with his wife Franca shows them at the airport, symbolically separated by a glass barrier through which they try to communicate. But on a physical level at least theirs is no arid relationship – Franca's warmth and passion for Pierre contrast with the relative coolness, verging on frigidity, of Nicole. Pierre, though, is now hopelessly immersed in his subconscious need to elevate the trivial-minded Nicole to the planes of perfection found only in fairy-tales: a characteristic he shares with other Truffaut heroes with a preference for fantasy over reality, like Coral in *La Mariée était en noir*, and of course Antoine Doinel, a similar slightly anachronistic dreamer with a taste for nineteenth-century literature. Returning from a clandestine encounter with Nicole at Orly, where his telegram to her declaring his love and the impossibility of living without her (a variation on Antoine's *pneumatique* in *Baisers Volés*) remains unposted, his sheepish apology to Franca for his earlier exasperation results in a passionate embrace which suggests that the marriage is far from dead. Pierre and Nicole, on the other hand, make a very

. . . and growing apart

ill-assorted couple. Their age difference is emphasized by his being content simply to watch her dance, and later by his encounter with a man only slightly older than himself, her father. The furtive nature of their affair is highlighted by their embarrassment when they take a room in a short-stay hotel.

Ironically, their conclusion that what they need is to escape from the pressures of Paris is exactly the solution suggested by Franca to the problem of her own deteriorating relationship with Pierre. The hilariously nightmarish sequence in Rheims, where Pierre is lecturing at the request of Clément, an old friend, is strategically placed at the centre of the film, where it leavens the surrounding atmosphere of hopelessness. Pierre's sense of being trapped and hounded grows moment by moment. He dashes from the official reception to buy stockings for Nicole (always a sign of male enslavement in Truffaut's world), then back to the assembled worthies of the town; survives a bad moment, along with the audience, when he thinks Nicole has come to seek him out in public (Truffaut playing with false clues –

again the Hitchcock influence); then is unable to shake off Clément after the lecture and suffers the agony of seeing Nicole propositioned in front of his nose without feeling honest or bold enough to tell Clément the truth of the situation. When the couple finally get away for their country idyll, his 'little girl', as Pierre has begun to call Nicole, feigns fatigue and later, as he clumsily caresses her, lies unresponsive on the bed. Her confession next day of having felt sullied on another occasion after experiencing sexual pleasure with a man, and of her ability to go without sex for a long time, reveals strangely dispassionate characteristics for the 'other woman' to possess; whereas, paradoxically, Franca's appetites are clearly fairly powerful. Pierre's preoccupation with photographing Nicole, on one occasion dashing frantically to sit beside her before the camera clicks, is symptomatic of his need to give a sense of permanence to the affair.

Returning to Paris, the lovers are muted. Pierre's feeling of guilt because his wife knows he has lied to her leads him to be excessively assertive when confronted with Franca's angry desolation. He accepts literally her wild suggestion that they should separate, glad of the opportunity to walk out at once. The slightly larger-than-life situation here; the shocked awareness of having gone too far to withdraw; the stubborn determination to go on playing out roles to the end – all this recurs in Antoine's break-up with his wife in *Domicile Conjugal*.

Pierre is blind to Nicole's increasingly casual treatment of him, and even the visit of her father does not reveal to him that a sort of protective paternalism is at the heart of his own feelings for her (the reverse of the coin of the Antoine-Fabienne relationship in *Baisers Volés*). Meanwhile Franca's attempt to get a temporary reconciliation with Pierre, accepted by him on a physical level but stubbornly resisted as a permanent solution, produces a violent reaction from her which anticipates the ending. Pierre's indirect marriage proposal is not accepted by Nicole, and he is hurt by her offer of a casual relationship instead. Life is closing in on Pierre; a point illustrated obliquely by the incident between Franca and the man who tries to pick her up just after she has seen the photographs of Pierre and Nicole, which is not a gratuitous comic interlude but reveals the dangerous extent of her anger, as well as illustrating the role of chance, again a key feature in this film.

Pierre and Nicole (Françoise Dorléac): obsessive photography and a furtive embrace

As in *Baisers Volés*, we can trace the role of chance in the film as a chain of fortuitous incidents on which the final outcome hinges. Pierre just catches the Lisbon plane which Nicole happens to be on; they happen to be staying at the same hotel and to take the lift together; Pierre casually keeps the book of matches on which he later sees the telephone number which Nicole has written; Franca finds the photographer's ticket when she has Pierre's jacket cleaned; and so on. Chance is of course the basis of much narrative film, but here Truffaut's skill in manipulating it is such that he makes the ending seem inevitable, paradoxically almost *because* chance can now be counted as a factor operating on the fate of the characters. The influence of Hitchcock, apparent in the climate of anxiety generated throughout, is nowhere more powerful than in the final sequence.

The justification for the shooting of Pierre by Franca, with which the film ends, has nothing to do with the fact that it is authenticated by a newspaper account of a similar *crime passionel* which Truffaut had read. It can be seen in terms of dramatic plausibility, as the only solution likely to appeal to the progressively hysterical mind of a spurned, passionate woman. In cinematic terms this final sequence is superbly manoeuvred. Pierre's dithering during the first telephone conversation with his wife's friend Odile about whether to begin again with Franca; the agony for the audience as his second phone call to Franca is delayed; Franca making her preparations with the rifle; the maid slowly and methodically checking that her mistress has left, and the thrill of horror that a murder is inevitably about to be committed. The ritual revenge of Franca produces its cathartic effect on murderer and audience alike.

11: Fahrenheit 451

After *La Peau Douce*, it was more than two years before Truffaut shot his next film, an adaptation of Ray Bradbury's science fiction novel *Fahrenheit 451*, which he had wanted to film for some years. The delay was caused mainly by difficulties in setting up the finance (Truffaut had bought the rights in 1962, then sold them to the American producer Lewis Allen, and had expected to make the film in America in 1964). The conditions of the final agreement specified a big budget studio production, to be shot in colour, in the English language and in England. Truffaut had hitherto made only relatively low budget, black and white films in French. His command of English was, and still is, limited, particularly in the context of a film whose centre of interest is its exploration of the problem of language. Yet Truffaut has often said that a film is a gamble, not a wager won in advance; and he badly wanted to examine the theme of linguistic and cultural deprivation in a bookless society. So he accepted the challenge and made the film. Ultimately, the problems proved overwhelming.

In Truffaut's adaptation, again in collaboration with Jean-Louis Richard, of Bradbury's novel, it is not the science fiction elements which interest him but the basic situation of a society in which books are banned and the job of firemen is to track them down and burn them. So Bradbury's Mechanical Hound, a machine which can be programmed to hunt and destroy human beings with lethal injections, does not appear in the film. Nor is there any mention of the total annihilation of cities in lightning wars, with the idea of society having to survive a new Dark Age. Truffaut's film, set in the very near future in an unspecified country, is more like an allegory or a moral tale (a feature of the novel, but to a lesser extent). The few futuristic elements, such as the search squad of flying men (a shot so casual that the lines by which they are suspended are clearly visible), the monorail and the television screens which fill a whole wall, are balanced by the late Sixties skirt lengths and even older fire-engines, while the telephones are fashionably antique. By playing down the science fiction emphasis, Truffaut has attempted to give the timelessness of the fairytale to a story which, as the Bradbury novel shows, really needed this extra dimension, afforded by the futuristic, Brave New World aspects, in order to sustain interest.

Neither the colour nor the big budget studio production gloss is a positive asset. Truffaut has said that he shot the film exactly as if it were in black and white, and apart from his fascination with filming flames and the impact of the strident red of the fire-engines, the film gains little from being in colour. True, the softer, more muted tones used for the gentle Book People contrast with the generally harsher colour elsewhere, but there is little sense of the systematic use of colour as a motif or as a demonstration of the theme. The artificiality of some of the studio sets would be credible only if it were reflected throughout the film and could be seen as a feature of the new, hygienic, plastic society. But the interpolation of natural decors, real houses and so on invalidates this possible justification. The use of Julie Christie in the dual roles of Linda, the fireman Montag's wife, and Clarisse, his girl-friend (which seems no more than a publicity gimmick), simply blurs the distinction between the two characters, contrary to the whole spirit of the novel. And the stubborn recalci-trance of Oskar Werner, who refused to accept Truffaut's view of the part of Montag, led (as Truffaut recounts in his published diary kept during the shooting) to the need to edit out a considerable part of his performance. Werner insisted on emphasizing the brutal, fascist elements in the part, whereas Truffaut took these as a point of departure and wanted to stress Montag's vulnerability, and in particular his growing receptivity to language and awakening to literature. One minor example of their quarrel (which reached the point of Truffaut using Werner's double on more than a few occasions) is visible in the apparent discontinuity between successive shots of Montag with hair of normal length and then crop-headed, despite attempts to conceal it by showing him wearing a helmet.

Fahrenheit 451: from illiteracy to the rediscovery of language (Oskar Werner)

But the major challenge which Truffaut failed to meet is basic to the success of the whole film: how to prevent the flat, functional characters, whose emotions have been dulled by state suppression of individual expression, from being swamped by a strongly dramatic situation; and how to generate interest in a relationship from which love – because of the paucity of language and hence of communication, arising in turn from the lack of books in particular and state policy in general – is absent. A Truffaut film which is not about love is as typical as a Hitchcock film without suspense. For Truffaut seems to me essentially a director of relationships, and if the film does not work on this level it is difficult for it to work at all.

The one level on which the film does largely work is as a study of the role of language. Truffaut's fascination with the concept of a world without the resonances of language in the form of the printed word, a world inhabited by zombies whose linguistic and thus emotional concepts have atrophied during a new Dark Age, proved difficult to convey in convincing cinematic terms. To succeed entirely, Truffaut would have had to show Montag's faltering development from this primitive state to one of linguistic fluency in a much more prolonged series of images, gradually increasing in rhythm – just as later he showed a much slower progress towards a more limited goal in *L'Enfant Sauvage*. The difference being of course that Montag's starting point is well beyond Victor's point of arrival. In *Fahrenheit 451* Montag is *re*discovering language and books as if for the first time, reawakening in himself a desire for a half-remembered previous state, hinted at in the novel by Clarisse's 'Was it always like this?' Victor in *L'Enfant Sauvage* is starting absolutely from scratch. The transition from semi-literacy to ecstatic fluency in *Fahrenheit 451* is on the whole not sufficiently gradual or awesome. In addition, the information clearly conveyed in the novel – that it is only in living memory that books have come to be banned, so that people do have a residual reading ability – has to be deduced in the film simply from the fact that there are so many books to be burned.

What does come through powerfully is Truffaut's reverence for books, epitomized in Montag's donning of what looks like a monastic habit before settling down to read *David Copperfield*. This reverence for the content of books extends to an obvious affection, which in any other context would verge on fetishism, for books as objects, the

110

touch, the look, the feel, even the smell of them. Under-educated himself and aware that he had 'missed something', Truffaut conveys his pain on seeing a book consumed by flames (anticipated by the Nazi book-burning in *Jules et Jim*) as if it were the incineration of a human being; and at a key moment in the film the two actually occur together. The intensity of this feeling for books eases our acceptance of the process reversed, whereby at the end of the film books are reincarnated as people – a device which out of context might appear naïve.

The film does suffer, however, from being made in the English language by a man who does not speak that language. Every other film by Truffaut is enhanced by his ear for the cadences of language, reflected either in the dialogue or the commentary. Every other film allows him scope for a certain amount of improvisation and flexibility with the spoken word, during the shooting and sometimes even at the post-synchronization stage. Truffaut's normal working method is to write up the next day's script the night before. This was obviously not possible with *Fahrenheit 451*, where he was obliged to adhere rigidly to the prearranged script, and the film is the poorer for it. A film whose theme of linguistic deprivation is already difficult enough to portray is seriously impaired by the linguistic deprivation of its director.

The opening sequence of successive zooms and close-ups of television aerials provides a visual background over which is 'super-imposed' the reading of the credits – a first indication of a media-dominated society where the printed word is banned. The terror inherent in a society in which firemen are judge, jury and executioner is emphasized at once by the pulsating music (by Bernard Herrmann, once Hitchcock's regular composer) as the firemen ruthlessly execute a typical lightning raid, culminating in the ritual public burning of the illegal books. The quasi-fascist aspect of the fire brigade – the crunching jackboots, the unholy zeal, the pleasure in destruction – is noted in passing. But since the central theme is not an anti-censorship protest, nor – despite Werner's attempted interpretation – an anti-Nazi manifesto, Truffaut does not labour the point.

Montag's meeting with his new neighbour Clarisse, in the mono-rail, provides further expository information: Fahrenheit 451 is the temperature at which book paper ignites; and Montag regurgitates

all the conformist answers – yes, houses have always been fire-proof; yes, the fireman's job has always been to burn books, which are anti-social rubbish and make people unhappy; no, he is not interested in reading the books he burns, and anyway it is forbidden; of course he is happy. But the impact of this encounter is less powerful than in the novel, where Clarisse, in the individuality of her thinking and her spontaneous, simple happiness, much more clearly disturbs Montag. In the film the contrast between the life-force (Clarisse) and the death-force (Linda) is muted by Truffaut's wish to avoid stereotypes, and also by his instinctive playing down of extremes (which he regards as a weakness in *La Sirène du Mississippi*); but this contrast needs to be emphasized here if Clarisse is to be more than a slightly unorthodox pretty girl next door. This lack of contrast may be partly explained by the difficulty for one actress in conveying the emotional range of the two parts; which may also account for the disappearance of the age gap between the two women – in the novel Linda is thirty and Clarisse only sixteen.

Television plays an insidious role in promoting and sustaining a society of mindless hedonists, because of its dominant position as a spurious 'member of the family' in every home. The illusion of intimacy and two-way communication provided by pauses in television plays for gaps in the dialogue to be filled in by twenty thousand Lindas all over the country – who are all then told that they are absolutely marvellous – is as near to real emotions as the nationwide televiewing 'cousins' will ever get. The normal isolation of married couples in bed in Truffaut's films is here pushed to extremes, as Montag reads his strip cartoons while Linda listens to non-stop radio with individual earphones. Linda's overdose of sleeping pills is treated as a routine case by the matey stomach-pump operators. It also allows an opportunity for a kind of clinical rape by machine as her body is stripped by the men to the accompaniment of their bawdy remarks. More voyeuristic satisfaction for the audience is provided by Linda's subsequent frolicsome seduction of Montag, reminiscent of a similar moment (also with Oskar Werner) in *Jules et Jim* and again showing the woman taking the initiative. And the general theme of a society deprived of love is illustrated by shots in the monorail sequence – seen from Montag's viewpoint – of women caressing themselves in solitary compensation.

Montag's clandestine reading of *David Copperfield* marks the

113

'As if it were the incineration of a human being': the lady burns with her books (Bee Duffell)

'A society of mindless hedonists': television as a member of the family

beginning of his rebellion. He learns of Clarisse's expulsion from her job as a schoolteacher, because of her unorthodox thinking; then later a scene showing an informant furtively circling round an 'information box' somewhat obviously signposts Linda's denunciation of Montag. His discovery that 'behind each of these books there is a man' leads to the climactic self-immolation scene, where an old woman sets fire to herself amidst her books, dismissed by the enigmatic fire chief because they are fiction, or written by philosophers who are idiots since they never agree, or because they have a socially divisive effect. The role of the fire chief (sinisterly played by Cyril Cusack) is rather ambiguous. There is a good deal of genial sadism in his treatment of Montag, but his own wide knowledge of books suggests possibly over-zealous reading habits in his youth – from the corrupting effects of which he is now pledged to protect society. The passion with which he discusses books, even if he subsequently denounces them, is indicative of the double-think of censorship: dangerous pleasures are accessible only to an incorruptible, self-

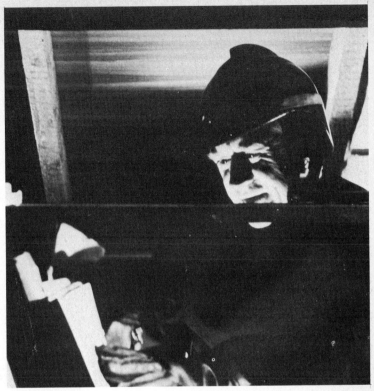
Dangerous pleasures: the fire chief finds some books (Cyril Cusack)

styled elite, who are themselves the arbiters of what may corrupt others. Since books are considered potentially subversive, the neat totalitarian solution is to burn them.

Montag's violent reaction to the concealment and frivolous diversions of television, and his reading aloud of *David Copperfield* which moves one of his wife's friends to tears, is seen by the women as further evidence that books make people unhappy. As Clarisse narrowly escapes the forces of repression, Montag's stunned realization that his last mission is to burn books in his own house turns to desperate joy as he destroys the whole house with his flame-gun and the fire chief with it. Television again distorts the gap between fact and fiction, providing vicarious excitement in a mock-up of Montag's death. A substitute is destroyed in front of the cameras, and the nation sees that 'a crime against society has been avenged'.

The escape of the real Montag to join the 'Book People', who live on the outskirts of towns and whose mission is to learn the contents of books by heart, completes the transition from author to book back to living person again, and is held up as a symbol for the survival of the human spirit. But there is a slight sense of over-explicitness in Truffaut's fairytale ending, as 'the first snows of winter' (during the shooting, by a happy accident) fall on a criss-crossing motley of people, some with walkie-talkie radio transmitters, reciting their books aloud in every tongue like a scene from the Tower of Babel. Innocence is suggested, but perhaps too innocently.

At any rate now, at the end of the film, the theoretical possibility of human contact, even love, exists. But Truffaut was not satisfied to leave his study of the relationship between language and emotion at this embryonic stage. And *Fahrenheit 451* can be seen, with hindsight, as an anticipation of the extended thesis of *L'Enfant Sauvage*.

12: La Mariée était en noir

From the fairytale land of *Fahrenheit 451*, where love may be dawning, we are transported to another far country, where the ice goddess slaughters five innocents who have slain her love. As this angel of death accomplishes her self-ordained task, we watch fascinated, having suspended not only our disbelief but also our capacity for moral judgment. Our progressive involvement with the success of her multiple murder mission is perhaps Truffaut's major achievement in *La Mariée était en noir*.

The film's basic premise is an unlikely gamble with audience reaction, more audacious even than Hitchcock's killing off of his heroine in the first part of *Psycho*, which causes the audience to switch horses in mid-course. Yet it pays off, and having lost his wager in *Fahrenheit 451* Truffaut wins this one. We do identify almost from the beginning with this inscrutable figure of vengeance, who is not merely unsympathetic in her emotionless efficiency but also morally unjustified in continuing her quest once the relative innocence of her victims has been established. We do accept her on Truffaut's terms – as a woman in whom all springs of humanity abruptly dried on one traumatic occasion, who died as a woman the moment her love died, yet who continues to function with terrifyingly mechanical obduracy in her chosen sphere. The truth emerges that if a film is cleverly enough shot, we will identify with anyone who so dominates the centre of attention.

La Mariée était en noir (*The Bride Wore Black*) clearly owes much to Hitchcock (it was made, incidentally, soon after the publication of Truffaut's Hitchcock book). It is adapted from the novel

117

The Bride Wore Black by William Irish (alias Cornell Woolrich) of *Rear Window* fame. The film's music is again by Bernard Herrmann, who wrote distinctive themes for each of the five carefully structured episodes. The audience is manipulated with Hitchcockian ease – the identification phenomenon itself is an impressive achievement – superbly illustrated by our expectation of a happy ending, which Truffaut deliberately contrives and then tantalizingly thwarts. Particularly Hitchcockian is the overall construction, with the resolution being indicated well before the end, as in *Vertigo*, thereby increasing, not diminishing, the suspense of anticipation. But despite the importance of these almost self-consciously Hitchcockian elements, which make the film the most overt of Truffaut's homages to this master, *La Mariée était en noir* differs significantly from most of Hitchcock's films in at least one major respect – the extent to which Truffaut makes the characters speak about anything but the plot. Thus the five victims are not entirely overwhelmed by the sheer mechanics of the construction, but command our sympathy as human beings. Truffaut has explained this humanity as part of his debt to Renoir, and has modestly described the film as another attempt to synthesize the best aspects of his two mentors. But under scrutiny, and in its development from Irish's fairly run-of-the-mill thriller, the originality of Truffaut's treatment emerges as much more than the total of the Hitchcock plus Renoir equation.

The transposition of the novel from America to a never-never land occasionally recognizable as France poses no problems. The main structural difference is in the film's rejection of the ponderous police enquiry section which Irish inserts at the end of each chapter. Truffaut does not bring in the police until after the third murder, and then not in a major role. The avenging woman, Julie Kohler in the film, appears and disappears at will, as befits a fairytale heroine. The progressive revelation, by flashbacks, of the motive for the murders is the key to the film's carefully controlled suspense. Some of the novel's irrelevant minor characters have been pared away; and Irish's fifth victim, a novelist, is replaced in the film by a car dealer, perhaps because of Truffaut's view (expressed in connection with *Domicile Conjugal*) that writers' lives are not the stuff of which films are made. The novel's highly tortuous final revelation dots the i's and crosses the t's in conventional thriller style; Truffaut avoids this by revealing the motivation of the heroine in mid-film, and thus

La Mariée était en noir: innocents to the slaughter

paradoxically, as in *Tirez sur le Pianiste*, maintains the suspense to the end.

The opening stills of Julie Kohler, naked and expressionless in artistic pose, flick by with machine-like precision, establishing her at the outset as a vision of womankind, statuesque and unattainable. The Wedding March is played on an organ; Julie attempts suicide; then, dressed all in black (and with a Hitchcockian emphasis on the angles of her suitcase, shots of her gloves, close-ups of her legs and so on) she simulates departure from the unknown town, and the way is clear for the action proper.

As the film proceeds, it resembles increasingly one woman's personal vendetta on behalf of all women against the masculine sex. In a reversal of the situation in *Les Mistons*, Julie hunts down five men, each representing different aspects of masculine behaviour towards women. The links between the five seem tenuous; but they all happened to be involved in the accidental shooting of David, Julie's husband of five minutes, as the wedding party stood on the church

119

steps. Julie's revenge mission is accomplished with an intransigence and an absolutism reminiscent of Jeanne Moreau's other major Truffaut role as Catherine in *Jules et Jim*. Like Catherine, she takes the initiative in manipulating vulnerable males. The difference between them is Julie's virginity, whereas Catherine lived according to her own code of sexual liberty. But both go 'to the end of themselves' and scorn the consequences. And both bring about the destruction of the men by whom they are surrounded.

Audience reaction to the death of Julie's first victim, inappropriately named Bliss, tends to be one of intrigued curiosity and mild surprise rather than of horror. Well, she killed him, after luring him on to a balcony by appealing to his gullibility and easily flattered vanity. Perhaps it will serve as a moral lesson to all such men-about-town who cannot withhold their services from an attractive and apparently inaccessible woman even during their own engagement celebrations. Perhaps Bliss' fiancée (Gilberte, like Jim's fiancée in *Jules et Jim*) has lost just another fickle male, whose casual collection of women is exceeded only by that of his friend, Corey. Their happy exchange of one of Truffaut's favourite aphorisms, 'When you've seen one, you've seen them all,' followed by Bliss' tape-recording of his fiancée crossing her legs in nylon stockings (another Truffaut fetish), marks them out as men for whom women are sexual objects. The humiliation of Corey by Julie, as she pours into a potted plant the glass of water he has brought her and then asks for another, is a small delight of revenge; and her pushing Bliss to his death, with the enigmatic phrase 'I am Julie Kohler' ringing in his ears, seems in the context little more than one woman's blow for liberation. We are interested but neutral.

Linked to her capacity for elusiveness is Julie's ability to transform herself by clothing, make-up and hair style into the type of woman most likely to appeal to each man in turn. So she establishes that Coral, her second victim, is a romantic who takes refuge from mediocre reality in dreams, which is the only world in which the ideal woman, for whom he is looking, exists. She engineers her meeting with him in a private box at a concert, where he is totally overwhelmed by her fairytale princess appearance, just like Antoine Doinel, smitten in a similar musical setting. Coral is presented throughout in a sympathetic light. He is a middle-aged bachelor, living alone in a cramped apartment; he pencils in the level of gin in

120

'The type of woman most likely to appeal . . .': Julie (Jeanne Moreau) adapts to her victims (Claude Rich, Jean-Claude Brialy; Michel Bouquet; Charles Denner)

121

his bottle daily, and does not notice that the maid waters it down; he looks into two mirrors as he carefully combs his hair back over his bald patch; he adores this vision of woman, calling her 'magical' and 'beautiful, too beautiful for me', as she dances in front of him, like Nicole for another middle-aged man in *La Peau Douce*. He is poignantly, pathetically in love, perhaps for the first and certainly the last time in his life. Our uneasiness that Julie should have awakened him to love, only to poison him coldly and watch him die in agony with a gratuitous sadism which transcends even her avenging *femme fatale* role, estranges us from her cause at this point; the more so after the further revelation of Coral's chance implication in the shooting, as the camera pans in flashback down the church steeple and the bridegroom clutches at his chest.

With the third victim, Morane, the pendulum begins to swing slightly the other way again, partly because of Julie's telephone call to the police to secure the release of the innocent schoolteacher suspect, partly because Truffaut develops the part of Morane to emphasize his least sympathetic aspects. Michel Lonsdale's interpretation splendidly anticipates his performance as Monsieur Tabard in *Baisers Volés*: a stolid, affluent, self-made politician who, like Antoine's father in *Les Quatre Cents Coups*, tries to instil into his child that there are winners and losers in life's rat race and the race begins at school. So he seeks to extract from Julie, in her guise as his son's teacher, her criteria for awarding stars for progress. Like Monsieur Darbon in *Antoine et Colette*, he needs to reassure himself that his own lack of stars at school has not hindered him in life. His hypocrisy and lechery are brilliantly conveyed in the short sequence which begins with his injunction to his son not to forget to say his prayers as he is put to bed. Then, as a violent storm erupts outside, he slyly decides that since his wife will now have reached her mother's and since, as he blindly imagines, women 'usually go for politicians', he will perhaps 'forget France for an hour . . .'

Julie's explanation of her motives, recalled by a sudden peal of thunder like the fatal rifle shot, is accompanied by the most detailed flashback so far, showing through the telescopic rifle sights exactly how the accident on the church steps happened. Her key phrase – 'For you it's an old story, for me it recurs every night' – prefaces her monologue about her pure, childhood love for David, shown with slow-motion shots of them in white playing together as children. This

'The thrill of anticipation': Julie in prison

account of the shattering of innocence occurs while Morane is slowly choking to death in the cupboard in which she has sealed him – during an innocent children's game. It recalls Plyne's monologue on the sullying of pure love in *Tirez sur le Pianiste*, delivered while he is squeezing Charlie's head in a stranglehold. But this doing to death of victims who are now seen to be innocent, or at most only marginally guilty, is not sufficient to purge Julie of her pain. The audience sympathizes with her now in the intensity of her suffering, likes her for her humanity in not allowing the teacher to suffer in her place, and fears for her safety as the arrival of Corey, just as she is departing from the airport, renders her for the first time vulnerable, a fugitive and potential victim herself. Pausing only to strengthen her faltering resolve at the confessional, and feeling now 'neither fear nor remorse', Julie resumes her mission, but is thwarted in her attempt to kill the car-dealer, Delvaux, by his untimely arrest and imprisonment.

In the fifth encounter, with the artist Fergus, Truffaut really gives his taste for audience manipulation full rein. The symbolism of

Julie's posing for him as Diane the Huntress needs no emphasis. This connoisseur of women is nevertheless predictably ensnared by the chaste, inviolate goddess. Minor tremors of apprehension inspired by the reappearance of Corey, who is 'sure he's seen Julie somewhere before', are quelled by the laughter which greets this stock phrase and also his next bit of patter about all women being whores 'except my mother, who is a saint', and then, 'When you've seen one . . .' But all hope of a 'happy' ending, threatened by two false climaxes as Julie's arrow quivers on her bow, is finally thwarted. Corey's sudden recall of memory, triggered off when he pours a drink into a potted plant, is too late to save Fergus from martyrdom, his heart pierced by an arrow.

Our reproach of Truffaut for having thus apparently misled us is soon replaced by our identification with Julie in the final accomplishment of her task. The thrill of anticipation, as we follow the progress of the food trolley from the female to the male block in the prison where she has deliberately allowed herself to be taken, is a masterfully prolonged moment of suspense. We have approved of her appropriating the huge vegetable knife; we now await nervously the victim's scream in the moment of silence which precedes the sudden eruption of the Wedding March, played on the organ, as Truffaut holds the final shot of the prison corridor. Our final identification with Julie is complete.

13: La Sirène du Mississippi

Inside any Irish tale there may lurk a bigger one. Take for example the episode with the pathetic bachelor, Coral, in *The Bride Wore Black*, blow it up, and you have something like Irish's *Waltz into Darkness*, or *La Sirène du Mississippi* in the French translation on which Truffaut's film is based. The significance of the Mississippi half of the title is lost in Truffaut's version, where the action is transferred from the American Deep South to the French island of Réunion and mainland France. Rather unsatisfactorily, Truffaut simply gives the name 'La Sirène du Mississippi' to the boat which brings Louis' bride-to-be to the island, thereby seeming to attribute to it an importance which it does not in fact have in the film. The title is presumably retained because 'Sirène' is an appropriate word to describe yet another wrecker of men.

If Louis in the film is unconvincingly snatched from his last waltz into the ultimate darkness, the fate which awaits him in the novel, it is because of Truffaut's views on what constitutes an acceptable cinematic ending. 'You must never end a spectacle on a downward curve. Life may descend into degradation, old age and death, but a spectacle must exalt and uplift.' Hence the preponderance of guardedly 'open endings' in Truffaut, with *La Peau Douce* as the only example of finality. Even *Tirez sur le Pianiste* and *Jules et Jim* imply at least the possibility that the upward curve might be about to begin.

The film faithfully respects the construction and proportions of the novel. The events portrayed are almost identical with those in the novel, as are the appearances, disappearances and reappearances of

125

the main characters. But rather than attempt a literal adaptation of a very long novel, Truffaut reproduces its essence by filming representative scenes. In the process, the extreme contrast between the ruthless female and the weak, naïve male is modified. Truffaut accepts Irish's conventional Hollywood thriller framework, but within it he is free to speak once again about love, as he does in all his films. Louis and Marion, though involved in an abnormal situation, are a modern couple whose fluctuating relationship is not intrinsically different in kind, though quite different in degree, from that of the Doinels in *Domicile Conjugal*. Truffaut has called his film the story of 'a degradation, by love', but it is a pale reflection of the long line of cinematic antecedents which he intended to emulate, from Sternberg's *Blue Angel* via Renoir's *La Chienne* to Godard's *A Bout de Souffle* and *Pierrot le Fou* (Jean-Paul Belmondo appears in both these Godard films and in Truffaut's film, and his downfall is brought about by Marianne in *Pierrot le Fou* and by Marion here). Within the strong dramatic situation Truffaut has scope to explore the intimacies of the couple relationship, in which for the first time there is no distracting 'other' man or woman. He can concentrate on the closeness and distances of their communication, their long silences, their frustrations and disillusionments and crises, all the shared experience which finally makes them indispensable to each other. He is free to write the dialogue for each scene the night before, as he prefers, and is helped by being able to shoot the film in chronological order. Above all, behind the flimsy mask, his self-revelation through the character of Louis is again as complete as in the Antoine Doinel cycle.

The opening credits sequence has echoes – visual, verbal and thematic – of a number of Truffaut's earlier films. The confusion of voices reading advertisements from the personal column of a newspaper recalls the babel at the end of *Fahrenheit 451*. The rapidly accelerating rhythm and intimacy of the correspondence between Louis and Julie Roussel develops the love by correspondence anecdote in *Jules et Jim*. The idea of any love being acceptable provided it relieves the solitude of this thirty-seven-year-old bachelor (the same age as Truffaut at the time of shooting) recalls the desperation of Coral in *La Mariée était en noir*. While the later revelation of the death of Louis' first love years before (on the eve of their wedding in the novel – seemingly an obsession with Irish) reflects the situation in *Tirez sur le Pianiste*.

La Sirène du Mississippi: the intimacies of the couple relationship (Jean-Paul Belmondo, Catherine Deneuve)

Truffaut claims that he dedicated the film to Renoir because whenever he was faced with a difficulty of improvisation he asked himself how Renoir would have solved it. There are also numerous references to Renoir throughout the film. A clip from *La Marseillaise* illustrates the moment in history (the 'Réunion') from which the island is said to get its name; though all this seems a pretty tenuous justification for some of the travelogue shots of the island, as if Truffaut had become aware for the first time of the potential of colour photography. (Yves Saint Laurent as costume adviser is another glossy, super-production irrelevancy which the film and Truffaut could well have done without.) Touches of truculent humour, typical of Renoir, such as the sequence in which Catherine Deneuve strips to the waist in an open sports car and a passing motorist drives into a post, are characteristic of Truffaut's frequently jocular asides on a theme – here women as the cause of men's downfall. One is reminded of the comic gangster's revenge quest against all women for the same reason in *Tirez sur le Pianiste*; and a similar scene features in the script of *La Peau Douce*, though it was not used in the final version. There is also a direct reference to Renoir's *Le Crime de Monsieur Lange* in the title of the film, *Arizona Jim*, which Louis goes to see in Aix. Again, the open ending purports to be a homage to the last shot of *La Grande Illusion*. And finally there is an obvious thematic link with *La Chienne*.

The scope of this chapter does not allow further exploration of all the other allusions and resonances which make of any Truffaut film a journey through its director's conscious and unconscious cinematic memory. The other two itineraries which this film traces are the geographical one, from Réunion to the Swiss frontier via Nice, Antibes, Aix and Lyon; and the psychological one, the progress of a passion which transcends the various stages of degradation through which it is purged, to emerge finally in a state of purity.

Everything which happens in the film is seen as usual from Louis' viewpoint, and his anxiety throughout is thus shared by the audience. From the moment when he initially fails to recognize 'Julie Roussel' among the passengers on the boat; through his acceptance of her explanation for her first 'adorable lie'; the ring which sticks on her finger during the marriage ceremony; their prolonged retention of the 'vous' form of address; his calling her paternally his 'little Julie' (cf. *La Peau Douce*); her preference for coffee, which she had claimed to dislike; her postponing the opening of her trunk and later writing to her sister — through all this we feel as much disquiet as Louis, and often, in good Hitchcockian style, Truffaut allows us to be one step ahead. Her indifference to the death of the canary which she had brought with her is not forgotten as we watch her 'innocently' seduce her husband, who finds her — again — 'adorable'. Later, after her unexplained beating up by a man unknown to us and Louis' insistence that his bank account be a joint one with her, he still finds her 'adorable', spells out that it means 'worthy of adoration', and, despite finding that she still has not written to her sister, tells her on the telephone that he loves her — ironically when he is on the edge of disaster. The conversation ends with a 'Me too' — 'Tenderly' — 'Me too' exchange of the kind which signifies a real love idyll in Truffaut's films (a similar conversation was removed from the final version of *La Peau Douce*, and one appears near the end of *Domicile Conjugal*).

Louis' belated realization that his bird has flown, with all his money, leads him to a ritualistic burning of her white underwear (later she is seen in a black dress) and a bitter revenge quest, spurred on by the arrival of Berthe, sister of the real Julie Roussel. To help him, Louis engages a private detective called Comolli (also the name of *Cahiers'* editor-in-chief), which allows Truffaut an opportunity to use some of the material left over from his researches into private detectives made for *Baisers Volés*; and also, in Comolli's fanatical determination to pursue his mission to the end, recalls the dedication of Julie Kohler in *La Mariée était en noir*. The central reconciliation scene — which begins with Louis finding himself unable to press the trigger to kill his wife, and ends, after he has heard her life story and learned that the real Julie Roussel was not ignorant of his wealth, with his discovery that his wife has fallen in love with him — recalls the opening anecdote in *Tirez sur le Pianiste*, where the man fell in love with his wife two years after their marriage.

A period of renewed intimacy, punctuated by a marital frolic and the use of the 'tu' mode of address, is a brief second honeymoon. 'It lasts so short a time. It happens only once and then goes away never to return,' says Irish. Truffaut expresses it by commenting on the hopeful idealists who try to establish 'definitive happiness' for themselves in seven lines of a newspaper advertisement, while Louis recognizes that his wife, whose real name turns out to be Marion, has brought him the 'provisional' (as in *Baisers Volés*) and that life is not

129

Fanatical determination: detective on the trail (Michel Bouquet); Julie and money; and (*opposite*) Louis poisoned so simple. It is chance, not choice; but the fireside scene of tender love in which Louis reverently touches Marion's features, again in profile, reveals that he has revised his preconceptions of love and is, as he says, 'enchanted in the full sense of the word' to know her. His subsequent shooting of Comolli is 'proof' to Marion that he has 'gone to the end of himself', and she at last wants him sexually (echoes of *Bonnie and Clyde* – Irish incidentally calls his heroine Bonnie – in the association between the revolver and masculine potency. One thinks also of Charlie's brothers in *Tirez sur le Pianiste*, who welcome him as 'one of them' because he has killed a man). But Louis still has vestiges of his previous social attitudes, which prevent him from appreciating Marion's scorn for 'men who work' and her hatred of the mediocrity of poverty.

The renewed intimacy lasts only as long as the money which Louis has brought from the sale of his shares in the factory to his partner. He is finally reduced to asserting his rights as Marion's husband by refusing to let her go from the chalet in the Alps (also the gangsters' hideout at the end of *Tirez sur le Pianiste*) where they have taken refuge from the police. He reads Balzac's *Le Peau de Chagrin*, with its warnings of 'excessive desires, intemperances, joys which kill, griefs which cause you to live too much; for evil is perhaps only a violent pleasure'; and then, from a comic strip *Snow White and the Seven Dwarfs*, he realizes that his wife is poisoning him for his insurance policy. Yet this perception prompts him to seek to forgive her, accept his fate, and ask her to finish him off – a parallel to her response to him when he first tracked her down after her disappearance from Réunion. And his assertion of his love for her, as she is and despite everything, awakens in her for the first time in her life the awareness that she loves him too.

Irish's couple find each other too late to save Louis' life. But Truffaut's couple exit hand-in-hand through the snow, heading for the Swiss frontier, growing dimmer and dimmer against the snow, and fading at last into silhouettes. This walk into the equivalent of an eternal sunset, however much it may strain our credulity, at least offers the possibility for continuing a love which Irish, with greater realism perhaps, found too strong and pure for this world.

14: L'Enfant Sauvage

Many of Truffaut's heroes start from a position inside society and move to a point somewhere on the outer edges – because society rejects them (as in the case of Antoine in *Les Quatre Cents Coups*), or because they in turn are driven by the force of events to reject society (Montag in *Fahrenheit 451*, Louis and Marion in *La Sirène du Mississippi*). In *L'Enfant Sauvage* the direction is reversed. Efforts are made to assimilate a dumb, partially deaf 'savage' into society. He must be broken in from his wild state, taught a verbal language and trained in social behaviour. For his own good, and also as a scientific experiment, the wild child is to be 'civilized', according to nineteenth-century notions of the process. Expressed here in one film are many of Truffaut's most fundamental preoccupations – the link between language and emotion; innocence versus learning; the individual versus society – with a possible key provided by the autobiographical thread.

Fahrenheit 451 was Truffaut's expression of the need for communication and the fragility of the means available. People are lost when they cannot talk to each other. Montag and Linda had only a debased, dead language; but their relationship is rich in comparison with the possibilities of human contact for the wild child, Victor, who even at the end of the film still has virtually no verbal language and can communicate his needs and affections only on a rudimentary level. His inner solitude is intact. As Léna says of Charlie in *Tirez sur le Pianiste*, 'Even when he's with someone, he is alone.'

Was the experiment worthwhile? Doctor Itard, who conducts it in the spirit of eighteenth-century rational enlightenment, appears

L'Enfant Sauvage: the wild child at bay (Jean-Pierre Cargol)

to think that it was. Despite temporary doubts about the 'sterile curiosity of men which snatched [Victor] from his innocent and happy life', he continues with the exercises and at the end of the film says he will go on doing so. More surprisingly, Truffaut appears to endorse Itard's view.

It is a matter of opinion whether Victor in his wild state was happy, the noble savage, or merely pitiful. The debate raises philosophical and sociological questions (about what is specifically, intrinsically 'human' in human nature; about how far supposedly 'human' emotions can be attributed to a near-animal; about whether there is a link between this idea and the 'pathetic fallacy' concept) which are beyond the scope of this book. The evidence in the opening sequence is inconclusive, though it does show a being apparently in tune with his natural habitat. What is certain is that his forcible removal from this environment leads him to experience feelings of nostalgia, rebellion and frustration for the first time. At the end of the film he is in limbo, neither savage nor man. Even if the experiment had been

The learning process

totally successful in curing Victor's dumbness and giving him a chance of some human contact, its basic premise could still be questioned. As it is, in the light of what Truffaut has called the experiment's 'partial success' (valid in scientific terms – but is Victor really better off?), it is difficult to share his optimism.

The key to Truffaut's attitude may lie in the fact that he was carried away by a sense of excitement about the learning process itself and did not fully examine the aim of the exercise. This may be partially explained again in terms of the strong autobiographical thread in the film. The important thing is not to be deceived by the decoy in the shape of Truffaut himself, appearing for the first time as an actor in his own film, into thinking that Truffaut the actor here equals Truffaut the man. For the key to the interpretation of Truffaut's self-revelation in this film arguably lies in the formula: Wild Child equals Truffaut (the man); Dr Itard (played by Truffaut the actor) equals André Bazin. According to this interpretation, the fascination of the film for Truffaut lies in the process of creation, or

Testing a sense of justice: Victor punished by his mentor (François Truffaut)

re-creation, itself, whereby a human being (himself) is freed from his shackles and becomes a new being. Without straining the parallel by a too literal comparison of all the details, Bazin, by moulding, instructing, guiding and judging Truffaut as a young man, fulfilled the Itard, surrogate father role in Truffaut's life. The unhappiness which was certainly an intrinsic part of Truffaut's own education — which he has repeatedly commented on elsewhere — now seems to be minimized by him and interpreted as a necessary part of the educative process. Perhaps for this reason Victor's original state is left ambiguous, and Truffaut is blind to the pessimism behind the apparently 'open' ending. *L'Enfant Sauvage*, like *Les Quatre Cents Coups*, seems above all autobiographical and only incidentally or even unintentionally a work of social criticism.

The opening dedication to Jean-Pierre Léaud is the first clue to the implications of the film. The subsequent caption, proclaiming the story's authenticity, refers to the fact that the film closely follows the *Mémoire et Rapport sur Victor de l'Aveyron*, written in 1801 and

1806 by Dr Jean Itard; though clearly on another level its claim to authenticity is that it is the most detailed self-portrait that Truffaut has yet produced. The prologue provides the necessary expository information before Truffaut can come to grips with the scenes of confrontation and the series of exercises which are the essence of the film.

The slow opening of the iris in the initial shot, showing a peasant woman gathering mushrooms in a forest, gradually reveals more of her surroundings. Our fear that she is not alone grows as cracklings and rustlings are heard on the soundtrack. The camera pans and tracks through sunlight and shadow made sinister by our apprehensions, like an animal scenting its prey. A louder cracking sound; a vague animal shape scratching at the earth and emitting curious grunts; panic and flight of the peasant; a long tracking shot to the object of her terror – a naked boy about twelve, his body covered in scars, very long black hair, face and body caked with dirt, quivering nostrils. He moves on all fours and stuffs his mouth with the abandoned mushrooms, lies full-length to drink from a stream, very quickly climbs a tree, the impression of animal-like speed being reinforced by the swift pan of the camera which follows him; cut to a shot of sunlight glistening through leafy treetops, then a close-up of the 'savage's' face seen through the leaves as he observes all that is going on, then scratches his back against the trunk. A very slow backward-tracking shot frames him as the sun gradually disappears, the final closing of the iris and total blacking out of the screen coinciding with the end of the camera movement.

This opening appeals to twentieth-century nostalgia for a mythical age of innocence, as depicted in Rousseau's 'happy savage', uncorrupted by society and thereby posing a threat to the values of that society by his very existence. (The sense of nostalgia is of course increased by Truffaut's use of the iris.) In particular, the association between happiness and nature, as in Renoir, is one of Truffaut's favourite themes, and there is a strong resemblance between the mobile woodland shots of sun glinting through foliage in this film and some of the most lyrical moments in *Jules et Jim*.

Initial audience sympathy for the child, which will be maintained throughout, is enhanced by the scenes of his capture by the peasants, whose boots and gaiters are often shown in menacing close-up. In contrast with the harsh animal world, and also that of the hostile and 'uncivilized' peasants, is the first shot of Dr Itard in his study, reading aloud about the child's capture and standing by an anatomical diagram of the human skull. His desire to examine the child in Paris, in order to determine 'the degree of intelligence and the nature of the ideas of an adolescent, deprived from childhood of all education because of having lived entirely separated from individuals of his own kind', is the first revelation of the essentially scientific nature of Itard's enquiry. The audience is kept informed of the reasons for each experiment by the use of readings (off) by Truffaut, in a fast, neutral monotone, from a newspaper or more often from Itard's diary; the special prose style of Itard's original reports is thus preserved, and also the essentially literary flavour of the linking passages which punctuate the film, as in *Jules et Jim* and later in *Les Deux Anglaises et le Continent*. The deliberate restraint in most of the shots of the doctor reflects the film's quasi-documentary style – appropriate to a scientific experiment; in contrast, the rare dramatic moments seem to be intensified. For once Truffaut seems scarcely conscious of audience reaction, immersed in his need to make the film for himself; so that in its austere classicism, with the camera often static and simply recording what happens in front of it, *L'Enfant Sauvage* is to some extent reminiscent of Straub's 'minimal' cinema.

Truffaut's easy condemnation of the more apparent excesses of eighteenth century society (such as the prison in which the child is tied up by his ankle, the jeering peasants who beat him, and the comic insert showing 'le tout Paris' flocking to see the spectacle of the child and inane comments in official reports about the likelihood of the savage's amazement at 'the beauties of the capital', together with the opinion that the child is insane) paves the way for his apparent acceptance of the assumptions about education on which Itard bases his approach. The child's transfer from prison to the Institute of Deaf Mutes in Paris, where he is catalogued like an object by Itard's colleague Pinel (and all this within the general prison of society), parallels Antoine Doinel's progress and institutional documentation in *Les Quatre Cents Coups*. The savage's indifference to loud noises but response to the cracking of a nut is recorded, and Itard theorizes that his dumbness is not inherent but induced by his isolation from society. The experiment with the mirror and the apple, in which the child finally understands and snatches the real fruit, seems to Itard to reveal something of his educability; and this slight progress is significantly accompanied by a gentle woodwind theme.

The guided visit to this celebrated child, lorded over by the male nurse and punctuated by the child's biting of one of the visitors, is one of Truffaut's few concessions to the audience in what is otherwise a bleak if always fascinating film. Other scenes establish that the child will not eat from a bowl or sleep in a bed, but seems happy playing in the garden in a torrential storm and drinking in the rain. Itard succeeds in gaining responsibility for the child, and with the aid of his housekeeper, Madame Guérin, tries to educate him in his house outside Paris. The remainder of the film is contained within the semi-documentary format of commentary, experiment, reaction, noting of progress made – all directed by Itard with apparent omniscience. He rarely questions the morality of what he is doing, but assumes as a point of departure that the 'education' he is inculcating into the child is of itself good, and therefore that the suffering and anguish which the child undergoes in this crash civilization course is justified because it is for his own good. Itard is a man of his times, whose application of the principles of scientific rationalism to this human specimen is imbued with a spirit of fervent curiosity which often seems stronger than his humanism. He may rationalize his apparent near-cruelty as kindness in disguise, but it is left to Mme Guérin and her simple maternal affection to provide the child with the real milk of human kindness. Meanwhile Itard is captivated, and exalted by every sign of the child's 'progress'.

Everything the child does is for the first time; the process is like witnessing the re-enactment of key episodes in the history of the human race. First, physical actions: unimportant, even trivial in isolation, but in this context cumulatively affecting. His hair, toenails and fingernails are cut, his shoulders are gradually straightened; he never weeps (which Itard interprets as a sign of the absence of any 'moral affection'), and he is insensitive to heat; he learns to walk upright, to drink soup from a bowl, but has his first fit of frustrated rebellion (one of the few scenes reminiscent of Penn's *The Miracle Worker*, despite their obvious similarity of theme) when he is made to wear shoes. As the softening-up process continues, he needs to wear clothes in order to keep warm. Itard's reward and punishment methods continue. The child's joy in being liberated for his daily walks in the country to see Itard's neighbour Lémeri is emotively evoked by the Vivaldi theme music, which highlights Itard's pleasure at the joyful moments of progress almost as if this chamber music for mandolin and flute were a gloss illustrating the pleasures of civilization.

The child's 'progress' continues, with a few relapses. He learns how to ask for milk, plays games requiring memory and concentration; and his apparent response to the sound 'o' brings one of the first overt acknowledgments that he is a human being when he is given the name Victor. The elaboration of a language, patiently and systematically but by pedagogic methods which might have been questionable even at the end of the eighteenth century, is certainly frustrating in a twentieth century educational context. There are signs that Victor's deafness is only partial, and one ecstatic moment reveals him banging a drum and ringing a bell in time with Itard. The exhausting rhythm of the exercises continues, unremittingly, though on one occasion Victor is so bored that he leaves the room and climbs a tree before his teacher notices his absence. The huge step from a drawing of an object to its alphabetic representation reduces Victor to another frenzy of frustration and, not surprisingly, when confronted with a set of letters carved in wood, to a fit of nervous rage verging on epilepsy. A later shot of him, face upturned again in the pouring rain, wild with joy, on which the iris closes, recalls the superficiality of the civilizing process and the strength of Victor's nostalgia for his former state. Yet he then shows tenderness to his master, taking Itard's hand and raising it to his eyes, forehead and then the whole of his face, in Truffaut's usual gesture signifying love. Itard next day locks him in a cupboard, and notes in his diary that Victor wept, for the first time. As Victor weeps, Itard's rage and regret for the 'sterile curiosity of men' is one of his rare moments of self-doubt. Victor finds solace in a return to the garden, face upturned as if worshipping the moon, then swaying round and gambolling on all fours.

The calm voice of Itard reacting to Victor's invention of a chalk holder ('Victor has just invented something. Victor is an inventor') seems to burst out triumphantly in this restrained setting, as if heralding a major accomplishment of the race. Then Victor's increasing skill in the fetching-of-objects game is accompanied by an acceleration in the music and the cutting, so that the whole sequence ends in another burst of triumph (the technique here recalls the 'coup

'Nostalgia for his former state': Victor baying at the moon

de foudre' sequence in *Antoine et Colette*). After this joyful moment, Itard's test of Victor's sense of justice – he punishes him unjustly, shuts him in the cupboard, and then rejoices when Victor bites him on his release, thus proving his elevation from the 'savage' to the 'moral' state – seems to be pushing the spirit of the scientific method to the limit.

Victor's final attempt to escape to freedom recalls that of Antoine at the end of *Les Quatre Cents Coups* in its poignancy and melancholy, and particularly in its revelation of Victor's solitude in an aerial shot of him running across a field of stubble towards the forest, from civilization to the wilds. But he has now grown unused to life in his old habitat, and so returns to Itard, who welcomes him with the acknowledgment that Victor is now in the intermediate state between the savage and the man, just as Antoine was suspended between adolescence and manhood. His calm final assertion – 'Tomorrow we will continue the exercises' – implies that the experiment was worth attempting; just as it was also worthwhile for

Truffaut to delve again into his own childhood. But this ending, as we have seen, is rather more 'open' than Truffaut realized.

The real Victor lived to the age of forty in Paris, and was able to perform simple, menial tasks. François Truffaut, forty-one this year (1973), continues to make films. In 1970, the same year as *L'Enfant Sauvage*, he made *Domicile Conjugal*. He then tried to take a long rest from films, which lasted only until the spring of 1971, by which time he had realized that quite simply he was unhappy when he was not making films. In addition, a project which he had been nurturing for a number of years now seemed ripe for fruition.

15: Les Deux Anglaises et le Continent

L'Enfant Sauvage is the summation of Truffaut's preoccupation with language, communication and the individual in society. *Domicile Conjugal* marks the culmination of the Antoine Doinel cycle (the proposed resuscitation of Antoine, incorporating extracts from existing films, can hardly develop the character much further). *Les Deux Anglaises et le Continent*, which Truffaut made in 1971, is another summit for him in the sphere of the literary and psychological love film.

A comparison with *Jules et Jim* makes itself immediately. The films are based on the only two novels written by Henri-Pierre Roché – *Jules et Jim* in 1953 and *Les Deux Anglaises et le Continent* in 1956 (his other work, *Don Juan*, was published under the pseudonym Jean Roc in 1921). The two novels are largely autobiographical, drawing on Roché's own diaries and notebooks. It is known, for instance, that the character of Jim in *Jules et Jim* was based largely on the author; and Roché uses a footnote in his second novel, at the point where the hero, Claude Roc, says he will write a book about his experiences one day, to explain that this was done fifty-three years later – in the present book. Truffaut uses this same footnote as a pretext for showing in the film the publication of Claude Roc's *Jérôme et Julien*, obviously a thinly disguised *Jules et Jim*.

Truffaut's film (called *Anne and Muriel* in English) is based not only on the novel but also on Roché's unpublished private diaries, to which he has access. For Roché the two novels were evidently fused in his mind, and the overlap between them is considerable. Truffaut's two films are similarly interpenetrated, and any discussion of *Les*

Deux Anglaises et le Continent must take account of its many echoes of *Jules et Jim*.

Truffaut has had to prune from the novel much more than in the case of *Jules et Jim*, in order again to concentrate attention on the central triangular relationship. There is no attempt, for instance, to evoke turn-of-the-century London, which figures prominently in the novel. The film was shot on location in Paris and Normandy, which supplies the wild beauty of the 'Welsh' countryside. On the few occasions when Truffaut has English people talking English, their conversations are slightly stilted; as was clear in *Fahrenheit 451*, Truffaut's ear for the spoken language fails him amid the unfamiliar Anglo-Saxon cadences, and he wisely reduces these English conversation scenes to a minimum. The relationship between the Frenchman ('the Continent') and the two English sisters, Anne and Muriel Brown, is more fully developed in the novel, as one would expect, and the same is true of the strong initial attraction between Claude and Anne. Again, some parts of the novel, such as the idea of being *un curieux* by profession and the tumultuous life-story of the non-stop Thérèse, have already been used in *Jules et Jim* and so are omitted here. Other incidents, such as Claude's first sexual experience – with Pilar in Madrid – are cut, perhaps because Truffaut might have thought them too explicit. The omission of Pilar is actually a positive asset – Muriel's reasons for refusing Claude initially are thus less specific – and the film gains in subtlety what it loses in explicitness. The obstacles which keep the characters apart in the film are rarely physical; more often it is their mental blocks and uncertainty about their feelings which prevent them from coming together. In this respect the film's atmosphere is very reminiscent of Gide's *La Porte Etroite* (one man loved by two sisters; self-sacrifice, self-deception and repressed sexuality all round; the frustration of any sexual consummation in the Gide and its postponement until too late in the Truffaut).

Details spelled out in the novel, like the Oedipal possessiveness of Claude's mother, are economically hinted at in the film; and all the novel's minor characters are pruned. On the other hand, Truffaut has preserved the flavour of the novel by retaining almost all the language, whether dialogue or reported speech, though it is often attributed to different characters or contexts. One occasion when the film might profitably have followed the novel occurs during the trial separation between Claude and Muriel. Roché effectively divides the page into two columns showing their simultaneously written diaries; Truffaut might have rendered the irony of the parallels and the increasing divergencies between the diaries by using the split screen device. His emphasis on the vagueness behind many of the characters' decisions is illustrated by Claude's conclusion that he wishes to live alone, influenced by his reading of Nietzsche in the novel but less clearly motivated in the film (though Claude does talk of his decision to create books rather than children). More generally, Truffaut reverses his usual emphasis on the role of chance. Here what happens is largely the result of choice, even if the basis for it is often inadequate or irrational and reflects the characters' timidity and inexperience.

The final consummation of the Claude/Muriel relationship is condensed in the film into a rapidly narrated epilogue. Having earlier given Anne a romantic death from tuberculosis (influenced, he says, by the example of Emily Brontë), Truffaut thus avoids the novel's crueller, if less spectacular, reasons for the fading of Claude's relationship with Anne – Anne's happy marriage and four children, an unthinkable ending for Truffaut.

The predominantly literary emphasis of the film is balanced by Truffaut's attention to colour in his recreation of *la belle époque*. The contrast between the interiors and the exteriors, as in *Jules et Jim*, is even more powerfully illustrated here by the colours, which reflect the tones of the Impressionist canvases of the period. Truffaut has enriched his study of the minutiae of desire, passion and tenderness with a happy marriage between words and images: a *Genou de Claire* filmed in delicate, sensual *and* functional tones.

Truffaut feels 'increasingly tempted by films which combine literature and cinema ... If *Fahrenheit 451* is a homage to all books, most of my films are homages to *a* book.' *Les Deux Anglaises et le Continent* endorses his view that 'if the beauty of a literary work lies in its prose, there is no reason not to let this prose be heard in the cinema'. The opening credits are superimposed over close-ups of the book cover, then one of the pages, several covers together, four covers on a shelf, then more pages, some annotated in the margin with Truffaut's shooting directions. A quotation from Claude's diary ('Muriel thought the account of our difficulties might help others') serves as a preface. The presence of the book will loom throughout, from this first moment until the last words.

The opening sequence, with quick cuts between Claude on the swing, his mother and the upturned faces of the watching children (as at the puppet show in *Les Quatre Cents Coups*), establishes the closeness of the mother-son bond. The first meeting between Anne and Claude contrasts the formality and timidity of the spoken words with the revelation of Claude's thoughts as Anne raises her veil: 'I had the impression of a modest and agreeable nudity.' This is the first example of the commentary – sometimes narrated by Truffaut, here spoken by Claude reading from his diary – which enriches the whole film. It is the first intimation of what Roché called the 'total frankness' of the intimate diaries, which Truffaut faithfully reproduces. The interior of the Roc house – brocade curtains, pictures in heavy, ornate frames, aspidistras, solid furniture, rich carpets and a preponderance of strong, dark colours – creates an atmosphere of opulent comfort which seems to weigh upon the characters, inhibiting spontaneity and prompting a stifling formality. Claude's mother is a brooding presence, her influence over him captured in a close-up of her face superimposed over an aerial shot of the countryside traversed by a train (reminiscent of *Jules et Jim*), and the comment that she 'raised no objections' to his going to stay with the Brown family in Wales. (In the novel his mother goes too.)

The vivid green of the grass tracks, and the sunlight and shadow of the Welsh beach, contrast sharply with the claustrophobic gloom of the interior of the Browns' cottage. Here the heavy mahogany bannisters, the dark blue walls at the head of the stairs and in Claude's bedroom, and the deep grey curtains in the dining room, provide a fitting background for the solid British reserve of Mrs Brown and the near-silence of the first meal, punctuated only by polite banalities and Claude's awareness of the absence of Muriel. After her appearance the following day, when she peeps at Claude with a kind of demure coquetry from under the bandage which protects her strained eyes, she is shown resolving not to be jealous of her sister, though there has so far been no indication (as there is in the book) that she has any need to be. A further hint of the future two plus one breakdown of the trio, with each sister alternating as the odd one out, is seen in the long shot of Anne, on whom the iris closes, from the viewpoint of the other two above the cottage in the gorse, where Claude is correcting Muriel's French intonation.

Subsequent sequences reveal Claude's gradual assimilation into the family ('I feel I have been adopted by the two sisters'), and disturbing indications that his feelings for them are more than fraternal. The sea's luminous blue and the vivid green of the grass make up another sensual Impressionist backcloth against which the grey stone of the cottage and the light shades of the three tennis players' clothing are picked out. 'The three became inseparable,' but their moments of complete harmony are fleeting. During a parlour game, reminiscent of Antoine's mime of a private detective in *Baisers Volés*, Claude's forfeit is to perform the 'nun's kiss', i.e. through the bars of a chair, on Anne. Gentle, almost pastoral music swells on the soundtrack; the flames of the fire are reflected in Muriel's dark spectacles as she averts her gaze; Claude kisses Anne tenderly on the cheek, the two of them silhouetted in profile against the flames (a similar moment in *La Sirène du Mississippi* signifies love). Another 'innocent' game, *citron pressé* in a cave, awakens further strange stirrings in Claude as he is sandwiched between the 'elastic backs' of the sisters. Mrs Brown's termination of this activity prefigures her more consequential intervention later.

During Claude's walk with Muriel at night, at the masochistic instigation of Anne, their disagreement on the nature of love (for Claude it is physical, for Muriel there is only true love) is lightened by her offer, and his refusal, of the archetypal apple. The next shot of the women of the house singing as they iron, with the sea glistening white in the morning light, evokes specifically Degas' 'Les Repasseuses', and more generally the lyrical, pastoral tradition from Renoir (*père et fils*) to Widerberg. A midnight conversation during which Claude actually strokes Muriel's hand and cheek, and explains to her that he is doing so 'because you come from the earth', offends Mrs Brown's English sense of decorum. The effect of her admonishment of Claude, during which she refers to the future possibility of 'a stronger feeling' between Claude and Muriel, is ironically the exact opposite of her intentions.

The next scene is quintessential Truffaut. Strong, melodramatic music; rapid commentary reflecting the hero's tumultuous thoughts; a written declaration of love (cf. *Antoine et Colette* and *Baisers Volés*); visual representation of the passage of time between the

147

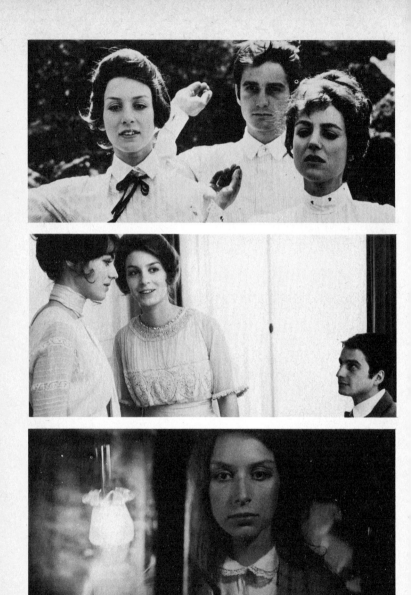

'I feel I have been adopted by the two sisters': Stacey Tendeter, Kika Markham and Jean-Pierre Léaud as *Les Deux Anglaises et le Continent*; (*below*) Muriel at her window delivery of the letter and the reply (successive shots of the Sacré Coeur in *Baisers Volés*, here a shot from Claude's viewpoint in a neighbour's cottage, to which he has been politely banished, of the Browns' cottage by night, with one light burning, then by day, with Anne and Muriel together in the garden). The gap between what is said and what is felt is illustrated by Muriel's refusal, 'We are brother and sister. I will never be your wife,' Anne's disbelief in the permanence of Muriel's sentiments, and Muriel's own ringingly romantic declaration, when she is alone, of her love for Claude.

The film telescopes the transition between Muriel's 'no' and her 'perhaps'. The strength of her emotions ('I am like a river which swells and subsides' – with rolling waves in the background) is frustratingly repressed by Claude's subservience to his mother's opinion and the acceptance by the couple of the decision of their neighbour, called in as arbitrator, that they should separate for a year. The anguish of all three of them and the contending forces in play are symbolically conveyed in one lengthy shot panning from Claude and his mother on the right via Anne in the centre to Muriel weeping on her mother's shoulder on the left, then all in one movement back to Anne again, who in turn looks to her left. The actual moment of separation is like a death. Muriel even says, 'Imagine, one of us might have died.' Claude's train draws away noisily, like the sound of the crematorium furnace in *Jules et Jim*.

Claude's mother narrates her idyllic love for his father in another setting worthy of an Impressionist canvas: tea out of doors, parasols and flowery hats, reflections in a lake, the ripples of boats and oars, which slip out of focus and merge into a hazy light. The main emphasis during the separation is on Claude, mounting art exhibitions and enjoying sexual love, thanks especially to a warm-voiced, seductive painter, another Truffaut siren reminiscent of Fabienne Tabard. The one incident depicting Muriel during this time gains in impact from its isolation. Grainy shots of her playing tennis with Anne, interspersed with sudden strident chords of extraterrestrial music and blinding zooms into the sun, show her hallucination, vibrant with light, of Claude's face across the net. Claude's letter of renunciation, setting forth his vocation as a bachelor writer and alluding to his 'women friends', plunges Muriel into prolonged agonies of fainting and jealousy. She declares that she is his wife, sister and friend (shades of Antoine Doinel) whether he understands

149

or not; she insists on absolute possession of Claude or nothing at all (like the 'stranger' in *Baisers Volés*); she has nightmares in the dark blue light of her bedroom (like those Louis has in *La Sirène du Mississippi*). Finally, a shot through a rain-soaked window shows her in the dark blue interior with a white lamp, vowing to write her diary for herself and never to marry, removing her spectacles and rubbing her eyes (like Sabine in *Jules et Jim*). A shot of the two sisters painting out of doors, in which the background of the sea is faded rapidly from light blue to a velvety midnight hue, recalls the Monets and the other canvases of the period which Claude has just been examining.

Another scene, this time reminiscent of the paintings of Manet – a high-angle shot of an open-air café surrounded by dark green foliage and patterns of sun and shadow – shows Claude with his mother and then 'discovering' Anne as if for the first time. With Muriel no longer an obstacle, Claude's only battle is with himself. In Anne's studio 'the mad idea came to him of taking Anne's breast in his hand', and he does so. Stendhal would have approved and so does Anne. His excitement at being the first man to touch Anne leads to their decision to spend a few days beside a Swiss lake. An extract transposed from Muriel's letters in the novel ('Let us live. We'll put the label on afterwards') serves as an introduction to the longest and most poignant tracking shot in the film. In the same slow tempo as the lyrically swelling music, the camera moves gently from right to left, across trees and with water constantly in the foreground, picks up Anne carrying a ladder, loses her behind the foliage, moves at her pace along the face of the waterside shack and round the corner to encompass her and Claude, then continues on the left with Anne seen through reeds along the water's edge – all in one uninterrupted flow. Their pastoral idyll has begun.

Truffaut's habitual *pudeur* permeates the ensuing scenes of increasing intimacy. Like Tristan and Isolde, they undress the first night on either side of an improvised curtain and sleep separately. Next morning, Claude outside the shack is the pretext for the camera, inside, to follow him through a 180° arc, in which luxuriant squares of green foliage framed by the windows alternate with the total blackness of the interior, as he moves towards Anne sculpting outside. She wants to make statues, not babies; he calls her curiosity sacred and prophesies that she will have many men. 'Their kisses

150

grew stronger.' The second night Anne learns that 'friends do not kiss each other on the lips with beating hearts', but her eagerness to lose her virginity is countered by her fear of doing so, and she sleeps quietly in Claude's arms. The third night, inspired by the flames of their log fire, Anne makes up her mind. The gentle humour of Claude's incredulous echoing of her decisions ('No curtain? No nightdress? No dress?') and her 'impossible red flannel underwear', gives way to tenderness as Claude asks her, naked in his bed, if she is really sure. As she draws to him, Truffaut slowly and discreetly fades to black and then equally slowly fades in the light. She has taken pleasure in his pleasure and in their intimacy, but 'it is not yet us'. Cut to a shot of the boathouse, landing stage, trees, shadows and deep blue of the lake, as Claude and Anne, silhouetted against the light, row away in separate boats. Claude wanted to prolong the idyll but Anne refused. 'They were free and it was beautiful.'

Three months later, when they meet again in Paris, Anne is in a state of wonder at her newfound womanhood: 'It was quite new for them both.' Anne is not jealous of Claude's other women, but strives to make an alternative life for herself, asking only, 'Love me as much as you can.' The comment that 'happiness is related with difficulty' anticipates the end of that happiness for Claude. Another lover enters Anne's life – a Russian publisher called Diurka – illustrated by a shot of Claude going upstairs to visit Anne (stairs feature prominently in Truffaut's films as the decor of many crises – Antoine in *Antoine et Colette*, and especially Christine in *Baisers Volés*). There is no reply to his knocks, and as Claude retraces his steps Truffaut fades to black. Next morning Claude tries to overcome his shock and manages to approve of Anne's actions, which are in accordance with their code; he advises her to go to Persia with Diurka and to listen only to the voice of her desire. Roché's succinct prose is heard in Claude's comment: 'Anne soon had two regular lovers. We both bore it badly. She, very well.' Then Truffaut's voice over: 'Before the departure for Persia, they had a farewell which lasted all night' (like the first kiss between Jim and Catherine in *Jules et Jim*).

The fortune-teller's prediction of unhappiness in love for Muriel, and a harmonious life with many men but with great danger for Anne, is followed by the arrival of a parcel for Claude containing Muriel's diary. Her intimate confession of shame at her habit of masturbation is spoken by her in a series of four intense close-ups, intercut with scenes illustrating the actions related. Claude is more curious than moved, regarding the whole account as potential material for a novel. His mother's death, conveyed visually, frees him from 'the most exclusive of all his women'. She lies in bed in a darkened room; suddenly very deep organ tones are heard, and the camera closes menacingly in on her; cut to a close-up of Claude wearing a black tie, and a background, which goes out of focus, of workmen removing a funeral drape from a building.

The film seems to gather momentum from this point. Claude sees Anne again in Paris, and then Muriel. He is frozen into inaction by his mental barriers: 'In Claude's thoughts Muriel was of a terrifying purity' (Truffaut's 'inviolate goddess' syndrome again). His confusion when *she* kisses *him* leads him to rush off in anguish, like Antoine in *Baisers Volés* after calling Fabienne 'Monsieur'. Muriel continues to take the initiative by inviting Claude to leave with her for the seaside. The repetition of Claude and Anne's decision that Muriel must be told about them, and Anne's protracted lingering over her account to her sister of her other two lovers, allows the audience to suffer in anticipation on Muriel's behalf. Her violent physical reaction to the knowledge that Claude is the third lover is accompanied by melodramatic music as she vomits and faints, the camera zooming in to the steps on which she strikes her head. Her letter of adieu is spoken by her in close-up, her weeping face superimposed over swiftly moving background shots of glittering water and trees.

Claude's own suffering is alleviated by his writing the story of his love for the two sisters. Its publication, as *Jérôme et Julien*, allows Truffaut to indulge his fascination for showing ponderous machinery (as in Louis' factory in *La Sirène du Mississippi*), here the manually operated printing press and the actual inking process. Claude's chance encounter (and such meetings are rare in this film) with Diurka, who works at the press, provides a moment of masculine complicity: they are both victims now. Like Truffaut (on his own admission) when he made the film, Claude now has 'the impression that it is the characters in the book who are going to suffer in (his) place'. Diurka accepts Claude's suggestion that the best way for him to find out why Anne broke off her engagement with a climber is to go and ask her, recalling the fairytale atmosphere of Jules and Jim's visit to the Greek statue and their resolution to follow any woman who looked like it.

Claude writes his love story

The next shot, showing Diurka amid the green grass, the grey rocks and the pale blue waters of the Welsh estuary, is another Impressionist juxtaposition of complementary colours. Anne, who unbeknown to Diurka is dying of tuberculosis, agrees to be his, but a shot of her bedside medicine tray (like Louis' in *La Sirène du Mississippi*) is ominous. Diurka waits; the iris closes on Anne saying she will not now refuse to see a doctor; cut to a long shot of the cottage at night (recalling Claude's view of it much earlier) with one light burning. The light goes out, and the frame opens out from darkness with an iris shot of Diurka relating all this to Claude and adding Anne's terrifying phrase, 'My mouth is full of earth.'

Soon after, Muriel is met by Claude on the waterfront at Calais, to lyrical musical accompaniment. As the couple move off, the screen is filled with shimmering pale blue reflections of the water on the boat's gleaming black side. The eroticism of the climactic seduction of Muriel, willed by her, is unique in Truffaut. It is not so much that he has finally succumbed to the general climate; indeed, what is actually shown even in this sequence is commendably discreet; but Truffaut has said that rather than a film on physical love he wanted to make 'a physical film on love'. Hence the importance of the fainting, vomiting, blood and tears. By comparison, in *Jules et Jim*, filmed at a distance in both space and time, the impact of the emotions is relatively diminished. Here the audience is made to experience the emotions with the characters, with a greater, almost physical immediacy. 'The violence of a love which has been for so long internal' wells up in Muriel. For Claude she is 'brand-new . . . aged thirty but looking like twenty . . . and he squeezed her like snow in his hands.' In contrast with the gentle tenderness of his first love encounter with Anne, here all is brutal passion as Claude unintentionally 'provides Muriel with a weapon to use against himself'. 'There was red upon her gold,' says Truffaut echoing Roché, and blood fills the screen. The rupture of Muriel's chastity is symbolic of the rupture of the ties that have bound her to Claude for seven years.

Next day she is dominant. She was resolved to come, see and conquer – 'I came to bury us.' Despite Claude's protests that she is now his wife, and his belated certainty that he loves her, she is now determined to leave. An 'amorous puritan' who is of a different race from Claude, she will not try to change him, nor will she stay with him, though she confesses, 'I can live without you as I can live without eyes or legs.' At the station two trains slowly cross in front of Claude and Muriel on the platform, each going in a different direction.

The epilogue, fifteen years later, relates that Mrs Brown is dead, and Muriel, married to a schoolteacher, has a daughter. A futile war has killed millions. Rodin's statue of Balzac, earlier praised by Claude, is now universally admired. Claude, bearded and bespectacled, walks in the garden of the Rodin museum and sees a party of English schoolgirls ('What if Muriel's daughter is among them?'). The camera circles the statue of 'Le Baiser'; Claude sees a reflection of his face and realizes he looks old; the film has depicted Roché's extraordinary love of life, but both Muriel and Anne have left Claude behind, and like Jules in *Jules et Jim* he is now alone. The final shot freezes on the stone doorposts and massive wooden door of the museum. We almost expect to hear Catherine singing again about the whirlwind of life.

16: Postscript: Une Belle Fille Comme Moi and La Nuit Américaine

Truffaut completed his twelfth feature, *Une Belle Fille Comme Moi*, in 1972; at the time of writing (September 1973) his thirteenth, *La Nuit Américaine*, has just opened in Paris. The following notes on both films are an attempt to keep pace with the director's output and to ensure that this present work is at least fleetingly topical.

In *Une Belle Fille Comme Moi* Truffaut accomplishes what he failed to achieve in *La Sirène du Mississippi*: the portrayal of a bitch. In the central role of a nymphomaniac, Bernadette Lafont waltzes through the film like a perverted version of the bride in *La Mariée était en noir*, whose mission is to use her sex appeal to exploit, not kill, her male victims. The one-against-five structure of *La Mariée*, itself an echo of the same pattern in *Les Mistons*, is here repeated.

In fact, repetition is unfortunately the film's keynote. There is very little new ground, and no sense of excitement generated by a fresh insight or an extension of Truffaut's usual preoccupations. Rather, the impression is of stalemate. The territory is familiar in every sense – Truffaut at home surrounded by the family he has created in the safe universe peopled by his own inventions. Names recur; actors and actresses reappear; conscious and perhaps even unconscious allusions to his own films proliferate (especially the attitudes to sexuality illustrated in *Tirez sur le Pianiste* and *La Mariée était en noir*); Hitchcock's influence, here *Psycho* and *Vertigo*, is again acknowledged; autobiographical details, such as the Villejuif reformatory and the joke on the psychiatrist of *Les Quatre Cents Coups* (here transformed into a naïve sociologist), abound. But the mixture does not jell; all seems stale and *déjà vu*. As in *Domicile*

Une Belle Fille Comme Moi: Truffaut directing Bernadette Lafont

Conjugal, Truffaut resorts to well-tried devices to solve old problems in familiar ways; and the result creaks.

Truffaut also reworked old themes in *Les Deux Anglaises et le Continent*, but in a way that seemed enriching. After this film a new departure seemed unnecessary and undesirable. As Muriel said to Claude, 'If you love someone, you love them as they are. You do not try to influence them. If you succeed, they will no longer be the same.' But the impression of sterility left by *Une Belle Fille Comme Moi* gave the lie to this optimism and left a big question mark against Truffaut's future development. One was reluctant to believe that he would be unable to emerge from this impasse. One hoped that *Une Belle Fille Comme Moi* would come to be seen as a work of transition, a tired résumé of Truffaut's past achievements, a necessary stopover point before the renewal of his creative inspiration.

Happily, *La Nuit Américaine* marks Truffaut's triumphant return to his best form. His total obsession with cinema finds its logical expression in this film about the making of a film. This is Truffaut's affectionate tribute to the cinema, a love song, a hymn to the crazy film industry and the eccentrics who work in it. Yet the film avoids eclecticism and conveys the impression of depicting, with warmth and intelligence, a surprisingly representative cross-section of humanity. Truffaut *en famille* again, surrounded by actors and film crew, makes us share his love of mankind like Renoir in *La Règle du Jeu*. Actors may be impossible but on or off the set they are constantly vulnerable, so they are also adorable and their whims are to be indulged. The message is again, as in *Baisers Volés*, that 'les gens sont formidables'.

In its freewheeling style and idiosyncratic tone, comprising Truffaut's quintessential tragi-comic mixture, the film recalls both *Baisers Volés* and *Tirez sur le Pianiste*. With its blend of humour and tenderness, it draws together both the 'American' and the 'French lyrical' strands in Truffaut's work. It is another Truffaut love story, another film in which the autobiographical thread is prominent. There is no division between the actors' lives and their work – and the actors here include Truffaut, virtually playing himself as the director of the film-within-the-film (his superb performance here as pacifier, cajoler and authority figure to his team of grown-up children recalls Dr Itard's handling of Victor in *L'Enfant Sauvage*, Truffaut's only other major acting role), and Jean-Pierre Léaud, who may also be playing himself, torn between the conflicting demands of the cinema and his private life.

Truffaut's treatment of the dichotomy between real life and its mirror image on the screen, with constant overlapping and interplay between the two, is both moving and funny. The film-within-a-film device, of course, has many famous theatrical and cinematic antecedents, from the Corneille of *L'Illusion Comique* and the Molière of *L'Impromptu de Versailles* through Pirandello, Fellini and Godard. 'La Nuit Américaine', as the film explains, is the device of filming 'day for night', whereby night scenes are shot in daylight through a filter. It is typical of the cinematic tricks of the trade and illusion-creating devices which this film simultaneously exploits and exposes.

The dedication to Dorothy and Lillian Gish is the first of the many homages with which the film abounds. The opening sequence then creates the illusion of reality only to shatter it at once with the revelation that we are watching the shooting of a film, as Truffaut

La Nuit Américaine: 'A man who needs a wife, mistress, nurse and little sister all in one': **Jean-Pierre Léaud** with (*above*) **Alexandra Stewart** and (*below*) **Dani**

plays in his usual fashion with our expectations. The tragic development, interspersed with humour, of the film-within-the-film (*Meet Pamela*) is paralleled by similar vicissitudes in the lives of the people working on the film. The apprentice Script-Girl (Liliane), the Make-Up Girl (Odile), the Props Man (Bernard) are given equal prominence with the stars – Séverine, the fading Hollywood actress, Alexandre, her fifty-year-old husband in the film, their son Alphonse (Jean-Pierre Léaud) and their daughter-in-law Julie, who plays Pamela, who is in love with Alexandre.

The whole film is a demonstration that film-making, in the words of Truffaut, both the actor and the man, is 'un métier formidable'. He compares it to a journey in a Western. 'At first you hope you will have a good trip. Then you just wonder if you will ever reach the end.' And later: 'Films go on like trains. They are more harmonious than life and there are no hold-ups. Personal problems no longer count. The cinema reigns' – this to the accompaniment of majestically low, swelling music.

The warmth and solidarity of the film-making team – they watch the rushes like a family watching home movies and later the group photograph resembles a family portrait – provides a temporary security for Truffaut. The importance of his craving is highlighted by the emphasis on the line 'Your parents invite us' (reminiscent of Antoine's adoptive family in *Antoine et Colette*). But the film also stresses the isolation of the director in his decision-making, pater familias role. Hence his symbolic wearing of the hearing-aid and the recurrent enigmatic flashback (similar to an episode in *Les Quatre Cents Coups* and based on Truffaut's own experience) of a solitary child's theft of stills of *Citizen Kane* from outside a cinema, followed by flight into deafness.

The incident in which Séverine can't remember her lines and asks if she can just say numbers with the correct dramatic emphasis – 'as with Federico' – is followed by frequent reassurances from Truffaut that it is not serious. In her confusion Séverine cannot tell if Odile is her make-up girl or a film actress playing the part of the maid (in fact she's both). The sequence works on a number of levels. It is funny and moving; it is an authentic portrayal of Truffaut's working method, his delicate handling of actors and his sympathy for them; and it illustrates the confusion between illusion and reality which runs through the film.

159

On set: Jean-Pierre Léaud, Jacqueline Bisset and Truffaut as the director

Illusion and reality: Valentina Cortese as Séverine, Jean-Pierre Aumont as Alexandre, Nike Arrighi as Odile

Another thread running through this and other films of Truffaut is illustrated jocularly by Alphonse's question 'Are women magical?' (echoes especially of *Tirez sur le Pianiste* and *Baisers Volés*). The humorous and inconclusive responses vary from 'No, but some are exceptional' to 'No, but their legs are', until Julie tells him that 'Everyone is magical, or not' and then spends the night with him, like Fabienne Tabard in the shortlived idyll in *Baisers Volés*. The discretion and delicacy with which this scene is filmed contrasts with the boisterous good humour of the many other casual sexual encounters in the film. Alphonse is a continuation of the Antoine Doinel of *Domicile Conjugal*, significantly described by his girlfriend Liliane, who deserts him for a stuntman, as 'a moody, spoilt child who will never be a man' and who 'needs a wife, mistress, nurse and little sister' all in one.

Echoes of Catherine's 'whirlwind of life' song in *Jules et Jim* and an anticipation of Alexandre's death are contained in Séverine's observation 'Our life is funny. We meet; we work together; we make love and then – pouff, he is no longer there!' The sadness increases with Julie's remorse at Alphonse's revelation to her husband of her infidelity and her decision to live alone since 'life is disgusting'. The moment of muted optimism in the reconciliation with her husband is painfully mirrored (on the set) by Truffaut, following his routine of drawing upon actual conversation to form the basis of the next day's script. As Alphonse gently touches her nose by candlelight and assures her that life is not disgusting, the shattering news arrives of Alexandre's death in a car crash.

These events, as always in Truffaut's films, overshadow the ending; and, as usual, he tries to lighten the mood. The film is hastily terminated with Alphonse shooting Alexandre's double in the back, in a scene reminiscent of *Tirez sur le Pianiste*, involving a revolver twirling amidst snow (here produced artifically by machine) to fast musical accompaniment. Odile, who 'has known many men', and one of the camera crew, 'who has known few women', announce their marriage, but our memory of the unhappy relationship between Jules and Catherine in *Jules et Jim*, about whom the same words were used, colours our amusement. The film unit breaks up and the camera pulls up and away from the scene of their farewells, the final shot freezing and then spinning round, evoking yet again the whirlwind – or the merry-go-round? – of life.

Filmography

François Truffaut

Born Paris, 6 February 1932
In 1947 founded his own cine-club
Army service, 1951, discharged 1953
Through André Bazin began writing for *Cahiers du Cinéma*, 1953. Also wrote for *Arts, Cinémonde, Elle, Le Temps de Paris.*
Assistant to Roberto Rossellini, 1956. Worked on three scripts which were never filmed.

Truffaut appeared briefly as an actor in *Le Coup du Berger* (Jacques Rivette, 1957, as a passer-by) and *Tire au flanc* (Claude de Givray, 1961, as a prisoner). His production company, Les Films du Carrosse, was involved in the production of *Le Testament d'Orphée* (Jean Cocteau, 1960), *Tire au Flanc* (Truffaut was supervising director and co-scriptwriter with Claude de Givray), *Paris nous appartient* (Jacques Rivette, 1960), and a number of short films, including *Le Scarabée d'Or* (Robert Lachenay, 1960), *Anne la Bonne* (1961), *La Fin du Voyage* (1961) and *La Vie d'Insectes* (Jean-Claude Roche, 1962). In 1964, he co-scripted *Mata Hari, Agent H-21*, directed by Jean-Louis Richard.

As a writer, Truffaut has also contributed to *France-Observateur, Les Lettres Françaises, Le Monde, Unifrance, Télérama, L'Express, Le Nouvel Observateur, L'Avant-scène du cinéma, Combat*, and to monographs on Roberto Rossellini (Seghers, Paris, 1961) and Jean-Luc Godard (Seghers, Paris, 1963). He has also published three books: *Le cinéma selon Hitchcock* (Robert Laffont, Paris, 1967; published in English as *Hitchcock* by Simon and Schuster, New York, 1967, and Secker and Warburg, London, 1968); *Les aventures d'Antoine Doinel* (Mercure de France, Paris, 1970: scripts and working notes for *Les Quatre Cents Coups, Antoine et Colette, Baisers Volés* and *Domicile Conjugal*); and *Jean Renoir* (Editions Champ Libre, Paris, 1971: a collection of essays by André Bazin, assembled by Truffaut).

163

Films

Une Visite (1955)

Director	François Truffaut
Script	François Truffaut
Photography	Jacques Rivette
Editors	Alain Resnais, François Truffaut

With: Florence Doniol-Valcroze, Jean-José Richer, Laura Mauri, Francis Cognany.

Shot on 16 mm in Jacques Doniol-Valcroze's apartment in Paris during 1955.

Les Mistons (1957)

Production Company	Les Films du Carrosse
Production Manager	Robert Lachenay
Director	François Truffaut
Assistant Directors	Claude de Givray, Alain Jeannel
Script	François Truffaut. Based on a short story in *Virginales* by Maurice Pons
Director of Photography	Jean Malige
Editor	Cécile Decugis
Music	Maurice Le Roux
Narrator	Michel François

Gérard Blain (*Gérard*), Bernadette Lafont (*Bernadette*), and 'les mistons'.

Filmed on location in Nîmes, August–September 1957. First shown at the Tours Film Festival (out of competition), November 1957; Paris, 3 March 1961; GB, 19 January 1961; USA, 1959. Running time, 26 min. (later cut by Truffaut to 17 min.).

Distributors: Les Films de la Pléiade (France), Gala (GB).

GB/US title: THE MISCHIEF MAKERS

Une Histoire d'Eau (1958)

Production Company	Les Films de la Pléiade
Producer	Pierre Braunberger
Production Manager	Roger Fleytoux
Directors	François Truffaut, Jean-Luc Godard
Script	Jean-Luc Godard

Director of Photography	Michel Latouche
Editor	Jean-Luc Godard
Sound	Jacques Maumont
Narrator	Jean-Luc Godard

Jean-Claude Brialy (*The Man*), Caroline Dim (*The Girl*).

Filmed on location in and around Paris, early Spring 1958 (filmed by Truffaut, completed by Godard). First shown in Paris, 3 March 1961. Running time, 18 min.

Distributors: Unidex (France), Connoisseur (GB).

Les Quatre Cents Coups (1959)

Production Company	Les Films du Carrosse/SEDIF
Production Manager	Georges Charlot
Director	François Truffaut
Assistant Director	Philippe de Broca
Script	François Truffaut
Adaptation	François Truffaut, Marcel Moussy
Dialogue	Marcel Moussy
Director of Photography	Henri Decaë (Dyaliscope)
Camera Operator	Jean Rabier
Editor	Marie-Josèph Yoyotte
Art Director	Bernard Evein
Music	Jean Constantin
Sound	Jean-Claude Marchetti

Jean-Pierre Léaud (*Antoine Doinel*), Albert Rémy (*M. Doinel*), Claire Maurier (*Mme Doinel*), Patrick Auffay (*René Bigey*), Georges Flamant (*M. Bigey*), Yvonne Claudie (*Mme Bigey*), Robert Beauvais (*School Director*), Pierre Repp (*Bécassine, the English teacher*), Guy Decomble (*Teacher*), Luc Andrieux (*Gym teacher*), Daniel Couturier, François Nocher and Richard Kanayan (*Children*), Claude Mansard (*Judge*), Jacques Monod (*Commissioner*), Marius Laurey (*Police clerk*), Henri Virlogeux (*Nightwatchman*), Christian Brocard (*Man with typewriter*), Jeanne Moreau (*Woman with dog*), Jean-Claude Brialy (*Man in street*), Jacques Demy (*Policeman*), François Truffaut (*Man in funfair*), Bouchon.

Filmed on location in Paris and Honfleur, 10 November 1958–5 January 1959. First shown at the Cannes Film Festival, May 1959; Paris, 3 June 1959; GB, 3 March 1960 (previously at London Film Festival, November 1959); USA, December 1959. Running time, 94 min. (released in 1967 in France in a longer version, running time 101 min.).

Distributors: Cocinor (France), Curzon (GB; currently distributed in a dubbed version by Gala), Zenith (USA).

Tirez sur le Pianiste (1960)

Production Company	Les Films de la Pléiade
Producer	Pierre Braunberger
Production Manager	Roger Fleytoux
Director	François Truffaut
Assistant Directors	Francis Cognany, Robert Bober
Script	François Truffaut, Marcel Moussy. Based on the novel *Down There* by David Goodis
Dialogue	François Truffaut
Director of Photography	Raoul Coutard (Dyaliscope)
Camera Operator	Claude Beausoleil
Editors	Cécile Decugis, Claudine Bouché
Art Director	Jacques Mély
Music	Georges Delerue
Songs:	
'Dialogues d'amoureux'	Félix Leclerc; sung by Félix Leclerc, Lucienne Vernay
'Framboise'	Bobby Lapointe; sung by Bobby Lapointe
Sound	Jacques Gallois

Charles Aznavour (*Edouard Saroyan/Charlie Kohler*), Marie Dubois (*Léna*), Nicole Berger (*Thérésa*), Albert Rémy (*Chico Saroyan*), Claude Mansard (*Momo*), Daniel Boulanger (*Ernest*), Michèle Mercier (*Clarisse*), Richard Kanayan (*Fido Saroyan*), Jean-Jacques Aslanian (*Richard Saroyan*), Serge Davri (*Plyne*), Claude Heymann (*Lars Schmeel*), Alex Joffé (*Stranger*), Catherine Lutz (*Mammy*), Bobby Lapointe (*Singer*).

Filmed in Paris and Le Sappey near Grenoble, 30 November 1959–22 January 1960 (some scenes re-shot during March 1960). First shown in Paris, 25 November 1960; GB, 8 December 1960 (previously at London Film Festival, 21 October 1960); USA, 24 July 1962. Running time, 80 min.

Distributors: Cocinor (France), Gala (GB), Astor (USA).
GB title: SHOOT THE PIANIST; US title: SHOOT THE PIANO PLAYER

Jules et Jim (1961)

Production Company	Les Films du Carrosse/SEDIF
Production Manager	Marcel Berbert
Director	François Truffaut
Assistant Directors	Georges Pellegrin, Robert Bober
Script	François Truffaut, Jean Gruault. Based on the novel by Henri-Pierre Roché
Director of Photography	Raoul Coutard (Franscope)
Camera Operator	Claude Beausoleil
Editor	Claudine Bouché

166

Music	Georges Delerue
Song:	
'Le Tourbillon'	Boris Bassiak; sung by Jeanne Moreau
Costumes	Fred Capel
Narrator	Michel Subor

Jeanne Moreau (*Catherine*), Oskar Werner (*Jules*), Henri Serre (*Jim*), Marie Dubois (*Thérèse*), Vanna Urbino (*Gilberte*), Sabine Haudepin (*Sabine*), Boris Bassiak (*Albert*), Kate Noëlle (*Birgitta*), Anny Nielsen (*Lucy*), Christiane Wagner (*Helga*), Jean-Louis Richard and Michel Varesano (*Customers in café*), Pierre Fabre (*Drunk in café*), Danielle Bassiak (*Albert's friend*), Bernard Largemains (*Merlin*), Elen Bober (*Mathilde*), Dominique Lacarrière (*Woman*).

Filmed in and around Paris, Alsace and St Paul de Vence, 10 April–3 June 1961. First shown in Paris, 23 January 1962; GB, 17 May 1962; USA, May 1962. Running time, 105 min.

Distributors: Cinédis (France); Gala (GB); Janus Films (USA).
GB/US title: JULES AND JIM

Antoine et Colette (episode in *L'Amour à Vingt Ans*) (1962)

Production Company	Ulysse Productions/Unitel
Producer	Pierre Roustang
Production Manager	Philippe Dussart
Director	François Truffaut
Artistic Adviser	Jean de Baroncelli
Assistant Director	Georges Pellegrin
Script	François Truffaut
Dialogue	Yvon Samuel
Director of Photography	Raoul Coutard (Franscope)
Camera Operator	Claude Beausoleil
Editor	Claudine Bouché
Music	Georges Delerue, Yvon Samuel (lyrics)
Lyrics	sung by Xavier Despras
Narrator	Henri Serre

Jean-Pierre Léaud (*Antoine Doinel*), Marie-France Pisier (*Colette*), François Darbon (*Colette's father*), Rosy Varte (*Colette's mother*), Patrick Auffay (*René*), Jean-François Adam (*Albert Tazzi*).

Filmed in Paris, November 1971. First shown in Paris and at Berlin Film Festival, 22 June 1962; GB, 10 September 1964; USA, March 1963.

Distributors: 20th Century-Fox (France/GB); Embassy (USA).
GB/US title: LOVE AT TWENTY

167

La Peau Douce (1964)

Production Company	Les Films du Carrosse/SEDIF
Production Manager	Marcel Berbert
Director	François Truffaut
Assistant Director	Jean-François Adam
Script	François Truffaut, Jean-Louis Richard
Dialogue	François Truffaut
Director of Photography	Raoul Coutard
Camera Operator	Claude Beausoleil
Editor	Claudine Bouché
Music	Georges Delerue

Jean Desailly (*Pierre Lachenay*), Françoise Dorléac (*Nicole Chomette*), Nelly Benedetti (*Franca Lachenay*), Daniel Ceccaldi (*Clément*), Laurence Badie (*Ingrid*), Jean Lanier (*Michel*), Paule Emanuele (*Odile*), Sabine Haudepin (*Sabine*), Gérard Poirot (*Franck*), Georges de Givray (*Nicole's Father*), Carnero (*Organiser at Lisbon*), Dominique Lacarrière (*Pierre's secretary*), Philippe Dumat (*Cinema Manager*), Maurice Garrel (*Bookseller*), Pierre Risch (*Canon*), Charles Lavialle (*Night porter at Hotel Michelet*), Mme Harlaut (*Mme Leloix*), Olivia Poli (*Mme Bontemps*), Catherine Duport (*Young girl at Rheims*), Thérésa Renouard (*Cashier*), Brigitte Zhendre-Laforest (*Linen delivery woman*), Jean-Louis Richard (*Man in street*).

Filmed in Paris, Orly, Rheims and Lisbon, 21 October–31 December 1963. First shown in Paris (and at Cannes Film Festival), 10 May 1964; GB, 5 November 1964; USA, October 1964. Running time, 115 min.

Distributors: Athos Films (France), Gala (GB), Cinema V (USA).
GB title: SILKEN SKIN; US title: THE SOFT SKIN

Fahrenheit 451 (1966)

Production Company	Anglo Enterprise/Vineyard Films
Producer	Lewis M. Allen
Associate Producer	Michael Delamar
Production Manager	Ian Lewis
Director	François Truffaut
Assistant Director	Bryan Coates
Script	François Truffaut. Based on the novel by Ray Bradbury
Additional Dialogue	David Rudkin, Helen Scott
Director of Photography	Nicolas Roeg
Colour Process	Technicolor
Camera Operator	Alex Thompson
Editor	Thom Noble
Design and Costume Consultant	Tony Walton

Art Director	Syd Cain
Special Effects	Bowie Films, Rank Films Processing Division, Charles Staffel
Music	Bernard Herrmann
Associate Costume Designer	Yvonne Blake
Sound Editor	Norman Wanstall
Sound Recordists	Bob McPhee, Gordon McCallum

Oskar Werner (*Montag*), Julie Christie (*Linda/Clarisse*), Cyril Cusack (*The Captain*), Anton Diffring (*Fabian*), Bee Duffell (*The Book-woman*), Gillian Lewis (*TV Announcer*), Jeremy Spenser (*The Man with the apple*), Ann Bell (*Doris*), Caroline Hunt (*Helen*), Anna Palk (*Jackie*), Roma Milne (*Neighbour*), Arthur Cox (*1st Male Nurse*), Eric Mason (*2nd Male Nurse*), Noel Davis and Donald Pickering (*TV Announcers*), Michael Mundell (*Stoneman*), Chris Williams (*Black*), Gillian Aldam (*Judoka woman*), Edward Kaye (*Judoka man*), Mark Lester (*1st small boy*), Kevin Elder (*2nd small boy*), Joan Francis (*Bar Telephonist*), Tom Watson (*Sergeant Instructor*), Alex Scott (*The Life of Henry Brulard*), Dennis Gilmore (*Martian Chronicles*), Fred Cox (*Pride*), Frank Cox (*Prejudice*), Michael Balfour (*Machiavelli's The Prince*), Judith Drynan (*Plato's Republic*), David Glover (*The Pickwick Papers*), Yvonne Blake (*The Jewish Question*), John Rae (*The Weir of Hermiston*), Earl Younger (*Nephew of The Weir of Hermiston*).

Filmed at Pinewood Studios, London, and on location near London (Roehampton, Black Park) and at Châteauneuf-sur-Loire, France, 10 January–28 April 1966. First shown in Paris, 16 September 1966 (previously at Venice Film Festival, September 1966); GB, 18 November 1966; USA, November 1966. Running time, 112 min.

Distributors: Rank (GB), Universal (France/USA).

La Mariée était en noir (1967)

Production Company	Les Films du Carrosse/Artistes Associés (Paris)/Dino De Laurentiis Cinematografica (Rome)
Producer	Marcel Berbert
Production Manager	Georges Charlot
Director	François Truffaut
Assistant Director	Jean Chayrou
Script	François Truffaut, Jean-Louis Richard. Based on the novel *The Bride Wore Black* by William Irish [Cornell Woolrich]
Director of Photography	Raoul Coutard
Colour Process	Eastman Colour
Camera Operator	Georges Liron
Editor	Claudine Bouché

Art Director	Pierre Guffroy
Music	Bernard Herrmann
Musical Director	André Girard
Sound	René Levert

Jeanne Moreau (*Julie Kohler*), Claude Rich (*Bliss*), Jean-Claude Brialy (*Corey*), Michel Bouquet (*Coral*), Michel Lonsdale (*René Morane*), Charles Denner (*Fergus*), Daniel Boulanger (*Delvaux*), Serge Rousseau (*David*), Alexandra Stewart (*Mlle Becker*), Christophe Bruno (*Cookie Morane*), Jacques Robiolles (*Charlie*), Luce Fabiole (*Julie's mother*), Sylvie Delannoy (*Mme Morane*), Jacqueline Raillard (*Maid*), Van Doude (*Inspector Fabri*), Paul Pavel (*Mechanic*), Gilles Quéant (*Examining Magistrate*), Maurice Garrel (*Plaintiff*), Frédérique and Renaud Fontanarosa (*Musicians*), Elisabeth Rey (*Julie as a child*), Jean-Pierre Rey (*David as a child*), Dominique Robier (*Sabine*), Michèle Viborel (*Gilberte, Bliss' fiancée*), Michèle Montfort (*Model*), Daniel Pommereulle (*Fergus' friend*).

Filmed in and around Paris and in Versailles, Chevilly-Larue, Senlis and Cannes, 16 May–24 July 1967. First shown in Paris, 17 April 1968; GB, 1 August 1968; USA, June 1968. Running time, 107 min.

Distributors: United Artists (France/GB), Lopert (USA).
GB/US title: THE BRIDE WORE BLACK

Baisers Volés (1968)

Production Company	Les Films du Carrosse/Les Productions Artistes Associés
Producer	Marcel Berbert
Production Manager	Claude Miler
Director	François Truffaut
Assistant Directors	Jean-José Richer, Alain Deschamps
Script	François Truffaut, Claude de Givray, Bernard Revon
Director of Photography	Denys Clerval
Colour Process	Eastman Colour
Camera Operator	Jean Chiabaut
Editor	Agnès Guillemot
Art Director	Claude Pignot
Music	Antoine Duhamel
Song: 'Que reste-t-il de nos amours?'	Charles Trenet; sung by Charles Trenet
Sound	René Levert

Jean-Pierre Léaud (*Antoine Doinel*), Delphine Seyrig (*Fabienne Tabard*), Claude Jade (*Christine Darbon*), Michel Lonsdale (*M. Tabard*), Harry Max (*M. Henri*), André Falcon (*M. Vidal*), Daniel Ceccaldi (*M. Darbon*), Claire Duhamel (*Mme Darbon*), Paul Pavel (*M. Julien*), Serge Rousseau (*The Stranger*), Catherine Lutz (*Mme Catherine*), Jacques Delord (*Conjuror*), Simono (*M. Albani*), Roger Trapp

170

Baisers Volés: chance encounter and cinematic memory

(*Hotel Manager*), Jacques Rispal (*M. Colin*), Martine Brochard (*Mme Colin*), Robert Cambourakis (*Mme Colin's lover*), Marie-France Pisier (*Colette Tazzi*), Jean-François Adam (*Albert Tazzi*), Christine Pellé (*Secretary at Blady agency*), Jacques Robiolles (*Writer*), François Darbon (*Adjutant*), Marcel Mercier and Joseph Merieau (*Men at garage*).

Filmed in and around Paris, 5 February–28 March 1968. First shown at the Avignon Film Festival, 14 August 1968; Paris, 6 September 1968; GB, 27 March 1969 (previously at London Film Festival, 4 December 1968); USA, February 1969. Running time, 91 min.

Distributors: United Artists (France/GB), Lopert Pictures (USA).
GB/US title: STOLEN KISSES

La Sirène du Mississippi (1969)

Production Company	Les Films du Carrosse/Les Productions Artistes Associés (Paris)/Produzioni Associate Delphos (Rome)
Producer	Marcel Berbert

Production Manager	Claude Miler
Director	François Truffaut
Assistant Director	Jean-José Richer
Script	François Truffaut. Based on the novel *Waltz into Darkness* by William Irish [Cornell Woolrich]
Director of Photography	Denys Clerval (Dyaliscope)
Colour Process	Eastman Colour
Camera Operator	Jean Chiabaut
Editor	Agnès Guillemot
Art Director	Claude Pignot
Music	Antoine Duhamel
Sound	René Levert

Jean-Paul Belmondo (*Louis Mahé*), Catherine Deneuve (*Julie Roussel/Marion*), Michel Bouquet (*Comolli*), Nelly Borgeaud (*Berthe Roussel*), Marcel Berbert (*Jardine*), Roland Thénot (*Richard*), Martine Ferrière (*Landlady*), Yves Drouhet.

Filmed in Réunion, Antibes, Aix-en-Provence, Lyon and near Grenoble, 2 December 1968–February 1969. First shown in Paris, 18 June 1969; GB, Edinburgh Film Festival, 6 September 1970; USA, April 1970. Running time, 123 min.

Distributors: United Artists (France/GB/USA).
US title: MISSISSIPPI MERMAID

L'Enfant Sauvage (1969)

Production Company	Les Films du Carrosse/Les Productions Artistes Associés
Producer	Marcel Berbert
Associate Producer	Christian Lentretien
Production Manager	Claude Miler
Director	François Truffaut
Assistant Director	Suzanne Schiffman
Script	François Truffaut, Jean Gruault. Based on *Mémoire et Rapport sur Victor de l'Aveyron* by Jean Itard (1806)
Director of Photography	Nestor Almendros
Camera Operator	Philippe Théaudière
Editor	Agnès Guillemot
Art Director	Jean Mandaroux
Music	Antonio Vivaldi; played by Michel Sanvoisin (recorder) and André Saint-Clivier (mandolin)
Musical Adviser	Antoine Duhamel
Costumes	Gitt Magrini
Sound	René Levert

172

Jean-Pierre Cargol (*Victor de l'Aveyron*), François Truffaut (*Dr Jean Itard*), Françoise Seignier (*Mme Guérin*), Jean Dasté (*Professor Philippe Pinel*), Pierre Fabre (*Orderly at Institute*), Paul Villé (*Rémy*), Claude Miler (*M. Lémeri*), Annie Miler (*Mme Lémeri*), René Levert (*Gendarme*), Jean Mandaroux (*Doctor attending Itard*), Nathan Miler (*Lémeri baby*), Mathieu Schiffman (*Mathieu*), Jean Gruault (*Visitor at Institute*), Robert Cambourakis, Gitt Magrini and Jean-François Stévenin (*Peasants*), Laura Truffaut, Eva Truffaut, Mathieu Schiffman, Guillaume Schiffman, Frédérique Dolbert, Eric Dolbert, Tounet Cargol, Dominique Levert and Mlle Théaudière (*Children at farm*).

Filmed at Aubiat in the Auvergne and in Paris, 7 July–1 September 1969. First shown in Paris, 25 February 1970; GB, 17 December 1970 (previously at London Film Festival, 18 November 1970); USA, New York Film Festival, 10 September 1970. Running time, 84 min.

Distributors: United Artists (France/GB/USA).
GB/US title: THE WILD CHILD

Domicile Conjugal (1970)

Production Company	Les Films du Carrosse/Valoria Films (Paris)/Fida Cinematografica (Rome)
Producer	Marcel Berbert
Production Manager	Claude Miler
Director	François Truffaut
Assistant Director	Suzanne Schiffman
Script	François Truffaut, Claude de Givray, Bernard Revon
Director of Photography	Nestor Almendros
Colour Process	Eastman Colour
Camera Operator	Emmanuel Machuel
Editor	Agnès Guillemot
Art Director	Jean Mandaroux
Music	Antoine Duhamel
Costumes	Françoise Tournafond
Sound	René Levert

Jean-Pierre Léaud (*Antoine Doinel*), Claude Jade (*Christine Doinel*), Hiroko Berghauer (*Kyoko*), Daniel Ceccaldi (*Lucien Darbon*), Claire Duhamel (*Mme Darbon*), Barbara Laage (*Monique*), Jacques Jouanneau (*Césarin*), Daniel Boulanger (*Tenor*), Sylvana Blasi (*Tenor's Wife*), Claude Véga (*The Strangler*), Pierre Fabre (*Office Romeo*), Billy Kearns (*M. Max, the boss*), Danièle Gérard (*Waitress*), Jacques Robiolles (*Sponger*), Yvon Lec (*Traffic Warden*), Pierre Maguelon (*Bistrot Customer*), Marie Irakane (*Concierge*), Ernest Menzer (*Little man*), Jacques Rispal (*Old solitary*), Guy Pierrault (*SOS employee*), Marcel Mercier and Joseph Merieau (*People in courtyard*), Christian de Tilière (*Senator*), Nicole Félix, Jérôme Richard and Marcel Berbert (*Employees in American company*), Marianne Piketti (*Violin pupil*), Annick Asty (*Violin pupil's mother*), Ada Lonati (*Mme Claude*), Nobuko Mati (*Kyoko's friend*), Iska Khan (*Kyoko's father*), Ryu Nakamura (*Japanese secretary*), Jacques Cottin (*M. Hulot*), Marie Dedieu (*Marie*).

Filmed in and around Paris, 22 January–18 March 1970. First shown in Paris, 1 September 1970; GB, 8 July 1971; USA, January 1971. Running time, 97 min.

Distributors: Valoria Films (France), Columbia (GB/USA).
GB/US title: BED AND BOARD

Les Deux Anglaises et le Continent (1971)

Production Company	Les Films du Carrosse/Cinetel
Producer	Marcel Berbert
Production Manager	Claude Miler
Director	François Truffaut
Assistant Director	Suzanne Schiffman
Script	François Truffaut, Jean Gruault. Based on the novel by Henri-Pierre Roché
Director of Photography	Nestor Almendros
Colour Process	Eastman Colour
Camera Operator	Jean-Claude Rivière
Editor	Yann Dedet
Art Director	Michel de Broin
Music	Georges Delerue
Costumes	Gitt Magrini
Sound	René Levert
Narrator	François Truffaut

Jean-Claude Léaud (*Claude Roc*), Kika Markham (*Anne Brown*), Stacey Tendeter (*Muriel Brown*), Sylvia Marriott (*Mrs Brown*), Marie Mansart (*Mme Roc*), Philippe Léotard (*Diurka*), Irène Tunc (*Ruta*), Mark Peterson (*Mr Flint*), David Markham (*Palmist*), Georges Delerue (*Claude's Business Agent*), Marcel Berbert (*Art dealer*), Annie Miler (*Monique de Montferrand*), Christine Pellé (*Claude's Secretary*), Jeanne Lobre (*Jeanne*), Marie Irakane (*Maid*), Jean-Claude Dolbert (*English policeman*), Anne Levaslot (*Muriel as a child*), Sophie Jeanne (*Clarisse*), René Gaillard (*Taxi driver*), Sophie Baker (*Friend in café*), Laura Truffaut, Eva Truffaut, Mathieu Schiffman and Guillaume Schiffman (*Children*).

Filmed in Normandy, Vivarais, Jura and around Paris, 28 April–13 July 1971. First shown in Paris, 26 November 1971; GB, 3 August 1972; USA, New York Film Festival, 11 October 1972. Running time, 108 min. (cut by French distributor from 132 min.).

Distributors: Valoria Films (France), Gala (GB).
GB title: ANNE AND MURIEL

174

Une Belle Fille Comme Moi (1972)

Production Company	Les Films du Carrosse/Columbia
Executive Producer	Marcel Berbert
Production Manager	Claude Miler
Director	François Truffaut
Assistant Director	Suzanne Schiffman
Script	Jean-Loup Dabadie, François Truffaut. Based on the novel *Such a Gorgeous Kid Like Me* by Henry Farrell
Director of Photography	Pierre William Glenn
Colour Process	Eastman Colour
Camera Operator	Walter Bal
Editor	Yann Dedet
Art Director	Jean-Pierre Kohut
Music	Georges Delerue
Costumes	Monique Dury
Sound	René Levert

Bernadette Lafont (*Camille Bliss*), Claude Brasseur (*M. Murène*), Charles Denner (*Arthur*), Guy Marchand (*Sam Golden*), André Dussollier (*Stanislas Previne*), Philippe Léotard (*Clovis Bliss*), Anne Kreis (*Hélène*), Gilberte Geniat (*Isobel Bliss*), Danièle Girard (*Florence Golden*), Martine Ferrière (*Prison Secretary*), Michel Delahaye (*M. Marchal*), Annick Fourgerie (*Schoolmistress*), Gaston Ouvrard (*Old Prison Warder*), Jacob Weizbluth (*Alphonse*).

Filmed in Béziers, Languedoc-Roussillon, 14 February–14 April 1972. First shown in Paris, 13 September 1972; GB, 26 June 1973; USA, March 1973. Running time, 100 mins.

Distributors: Columbia (France/USA), Gala (GB).
GB title: A GORGEOUS BIRD LIKE ME; US title: SUCH A GORGEOUS KID LIKE ME

La Nuit Américaine (1973)

Production Company	Les Films du Carrosse/PECF (Paris)/Produzione Internazionale Cinematografica (Rome)
Producer	Marcel Berbert
Production Manager	Claude Miler
Director	François Truffaut
Assistant Director	Suzanne Schiffman
Script	François Truffaut, Jean-Louis Richard, Suzanne Schiffman
Director of Photography	Pierre William Glenn
Colour Process	Eastman Colour
Editor	Yann Dedet

Art Director	Damien Lanfranchi
Costumes	Monique Dury
Sound	René Levert

Jacqueline Bisset (*Julie/Pamela*), Valentine Cortese (*Séverine*), Alexandra Stewart (*Stacey*), Jean-Pierre Aumont (*Alexandre*), Jean-Pierre Léaud (*Alphonse*), François Truffaut (*Ferrand*), Jean Champion (*Bertrand*), Nathalie Baye (*Joëlle*), Dani (*Assistant continuity girl*), Bernard Menez (*Property Man*), Nike Arrigh (*Odile*), Gaston Joly (*Gaston*), Jean Panisse (*Arthur*), Maurice Séveno (*TV reporter*), David Markham (*Dr Nelson*), Zénaïde Rossi (*Gaston's wife*), Christophe Vesque (*Boy*), Henry Graham and Marcel Berbert (*Insurers*).

Filmed at the Studio Victorine and on location in Nice, 25 September–December 1972. First shown in Paris, 24 May 1973; USA, New York Film Festival, 28 September 1973. Running time, 120 min.

Distributors: Columbia-Warner (France/GB), Warner Bros. (USA).
GB title: DAY FOR NIGHT

Acknowledgments

In London, I should like to thank Jan Dawson, Penelope Houston and David Wilson for their constructive criticism; the staff of the BFI Information Department and Library for their help; and Joan Stevens for her speedy typing.

In Paris, I am grateful to Christine Brierre and Lucette de Givray for documentation and stills; Claude de Givray for interviews and insights; Rui Nogueira for his cuttings and his invaluable opinion and advice; and of course François Truffaut for generously making himself available for numerous interviews and allowing me to be present during the shooting, rushes and previews of his last few films.

This book is dedicated to Lyn, who lived with it for two years.

Stills by courtesy of Les Films du Carrosse, Columbia-Warner, Gala, Rank, 20th Century-Fox, United Artists and the Stills Library of the National Film Archive, London.